Julia and the Moonbirds

Also by Mark Cornell and published by Ginninderra Press
A Journey To Glory

Mark Cornell

Julia and the Moonbirds

Julia and the Moonbirds
ISBN 978 1 76041 561 7
Copyright © text Mark Cornell 2018

First published 2018 by
GINNINDERRA PRESS
PO Box 3461 Port Adelaide 5015
www.ginninderrapress.com.au

Contents

1

Ocean child

The first time I met Julia King, she was drunk. Later on, she denied it, but how else could you explain her behaviour? With her arm around my shoulder, and breath fragrant with vodka and orange, she kept encouraging me. It was New Year's Eve and I'd just seen her perform. She was on the second-last float of the Portmagee parade. I was in the middle of the crowd in Sackville Street watching the floats sail by.

Poseidon opened our town's procession. I'd seen him earlier as I stepped out of my house; he was in his half-naked glory, bright green seaweed for hair and beard and clutching a trident in a bath being wheeled up Wishart Street by his mates. Julia was behind Miss Western District Potato Queen (young Sally Cassy dressed up in papier mâché as a giant spud). With Julia, you tended to hear her before you saw her.

Julia and her band, the Moonbirds, were doing a rough version of Van the Man's 'Gloria'. By rough, I mean a weird thing of noises and splendour. While Steve Weston, the drummer, pounded away on his pig skins, a change was just about to blow through; the way he played I couldn't tell if it was him or the rumble of thunder out on Bass Strait. Sue Sutcliffe was on bass, hiding behind thick black sunglasses with her back permanently turned against the audience. Alex Fitzsimmons attempted a lead guitar break which sounded like a tomcat with its knackers stuck in a vice. Then there was Julia.

She had thick, long, flowing red hair and a slight figure. What she lacked in size was made up by mojo. With her pointy nose and big dark brown eyes, she reminded me of the kestrels that flutter in the fields outside of town. Julia had a guitar which she kept swivelling aside like Elvis, and when she wasn't hovering on the edge of the float, she was jumping madly up and down on the top of the truck cabin. She had a powerful set of lungs for a little woman.

Julia loved to tease the crowd. Just when you thought 'Gloria' was finished, she'd crank it up again. While the old-timers of Portmagee didn't know what to make of her, the kids loved her. I watched as her mad little silhouette faded slowly into the dark end of Sackville Street. 'Gloria' was finally washed out by a thunderstorm.

I stood transfixed, smitten…knowing I never had a chance with her. For starters, there was the huge age gap of eighteen months. She was near eighteen; I was only sixteen-and-a-half. She was Portmagee High's chief trouble-maker; I usually stuck to the rules, especially since the death of my mother, Mary. But there I was, half embarrassed in the village green, with Julia's arm locked around me. The green was packed with farming families down from the Western District for a holiday, local yokels, and fishermen taking a break from the wild waters of Bass Strait.

Julia took a few swigs from her bottle then laughed out to a well-dressed farmer, 'Missing any of your girlfriends lately, cockie?' By girlfriends, Julia meant sheep. The more affluent of the Western District occasionally lost sheep to a gang of unknown shooters.

'If I had me gun on me now, I'd shoot you, you trouble-making little bitch.' The farmer gave her a look to kill.

A little stunned, Julia took another swig and, with a huge grin, gave him the two-fingered salute.

'Wendy tells me you've mastered six chords on the guitar, you clever boy.'

Wendy Chan was this incredibly spunky girl I sat next to in Social Studies. Her ancestors trudged from Robe to the Ballarat goldfields to avoid a tax the Victorian government tried to impose on Chinese immigrants. With her high cheekbones, smiley face and incredibly long legs, she was adorable and she was a close friend of Julia's who'd stayed down for a year because she loved boys and hated study. Wendy and I had incredible heart-to-hearts, but again I assumed that, like Julia, she was out of my league. Later on, at our high school break-up, she confessed that she loved me. God! Missed opportunities are the story of my life! I love heart-to-hearts with women; I had them all the time with my mum before the cancer took her away.

Waves of excitement flooded from my scalp to the extremities of my body when Julia ruffled my hair.

'She also tells me you have an exercise book full of lyrics. I'd love to see them, Shane!'

It was like she'd spoken to me from far away and with the combination of her touch and her interest in my inner world, I soared above Bass Strait to burst right through the thunderstorm and zoom straight up to the moon...

'Shaney, Shaney McCarthy,' someone whispered, summoning me back to New Year's Eve, 1969, Portmagee. What the hell do I say to this strong, spirited woman? She's notorious throughout the township for not putting up with any bullshit, especially from males.

'Um, yeah, Dad's taught me the chords and yeah, yeah you're welcome to look at my lyrics. I must warn you, though, I do write a lot of rubbish.'

'Let's go back to Wishart Street. I want to see what you can do and I'd like to see your lyrics.' Julia's face flared as she lit up a cigarette.

We huddled and dashed through the horizontal rain, Julia giggling as she linked her frozen fingers with mine. A flash of lightning lit up old Seacombe House Inn. Waves smashed into the rocks at nearby Pea Soup Beach.

'Brrr! The heavens have opened up. Do you want some of this?' Snuggling, she took the bottle out of her coat pocket and offered it to me.

I'd sneaked Dad's Fosters out of the fridge sometimes, but I'd never tried spirits before. 'Yeah, OK!' I replied, trying to put on a deep voice. It singed my gullet as it went down. I took a few more swigs then walked on air as we hit Wishart Street. 'Rain? What rain?' I blurted and Julia kept on laughing.

My two cats, Nugget and Midge, greeted us at the front door.

'Puddy tats! Oh, I love them, Shane!'

Rain-glistening Julia shone as my two black furry girls did their circle of eight dance around her ankles. She threw her drenched parka onto the floor and when she bent down to pat my girls, I discovered Julia had a tattoo at the base of her spine.

In the lounge room, I stoked up the logs Dad had left simmering for me. Yellow flames snaked up the hearth.

'Where's your Da and Mike?' Julia crouched down to explore our record collection.

'He's playing with his band in the Caledonian. Mike's gone with him. Dad's decided that seeing he's ten, he's old enough to appreciate his first New Year.'

'Whack oh the diddly oh! Let's party. *The White Album*!' Julia jumped up with glee and whacked the Beatles on. She turned the volume right up and danced to 'Back in the USSR'.

I couldn't resist her summons to dance.

'This album's brilliant. It's when the boys got back to the basics and swept away all that hippy shit!' she bellowed into my ear. 'That's what I want to do with the Moonbirds. I'm sick of fucking long-hairs sitting around listening to cosmic crap like at Woodstock. Rock 'n' roll's about raging.' She stretched her pale neck back and emptied the bottle. 'Don't worry, Shaney, I've got another.' She slipped it out of the pocket of her jeans. 'Want some ?'

'Don't mind if I do.' I took it out of her hand and gulped down a few mouthfuls.

When 'Dear Prudence' came on, I felt like I was floating inside a cloud and before I knew it we were leaning back on the couch together. But Nugget jumped onto Julia's lap to begin her settling down to sleep routine. Stupid interfering cat!

'Puss, puss, puss!' Julia's dark saucer eyes glistened as she scratched Nugget's chin.

My cat's purr was so loud it almost blocked out the sound of rain and that was something because Portmagee was putting on a summer hurricane. Our house creaked like an old sailing ship out at sea. Bass Strait roared. Nervously, I tapped my foot along to 'Happiness is a Warm Gun'.

Julia turned her rain-streaked head towards me. 'Wendy said you were gorgeous. She's right. Now how about showing me what you can do with your guitar?' She leant over to brush the thick fringe back from my forehead.

As I stood up and glided into my bedroom to get my acoustic guitar, I discovered I'd entered into a wonderful vodka haze. Christ, I was a superhero! Play a few songs? Pah! I'll show her! Bloody Moonbirds are a pack of amateurs!

The fire flared as I tossed in a few thick branches. I'm a magician! A conjurer! I tuned my guitar then played her 'Only the Lonely'. Julia gave me a few more swigs and I went onto 'Peggy Sue' and 'That'll be the Day'. Sing! Sing! Sing! I could go all bloody night. Give me some more vodka, Julia! You know how to get to my very core, woman! I produced my exercise book from underneath the couch and showed her my lyrics. She went silent and my heart swelled up to my throat. Apart from Mary, she was the first person ever to see my work. Christ, what am I doing? Ugh! She's taking forever. She's probably embarrassed! I mean, it's pretty basic stuff!

She raised her head. Was that a tear in her eye? 'Your words are beautiful, Shane…you obviously miss Mary.'

'She's all I write about.' Now I was the one close to holding back the tears. I slowly shook my head. 'She was my soulmate. She was the only other person on this planet who really knew me. The conversations we used to have! God bless her, she always encouraged my writing. Like you she took my words seriously. You see, I get a lot of shit from the dickheads at school who reckon I'm a poof because I write.'

'Which arseholes give you a hard time?' Julia's chest expanded.

'Ah, you know, that barbarian Paul Evans, that creep Heath Sexton, that brainless wonder Neville Whitely and that prick Leigh Adamson.

Every chance those arseholes get they love to bash me up behind the portables!' I gazed down at the fire.

'What's your Da doing about it?'

'Bugger all. He thinks it's character-forming. You know…all that macho bullshit!'

'Bastards like that shouldn't get away with it, Shane.'

Julia's red face reminded me of the sunsets you get here sometimes when the sky's full of dust. The sun swells to twice its normal size. To this day, the sight of her wrathful face haunts me.

We drank on in silence until Julia invited me to put my head on her lap.

She combed her thin white fingers through my hair. 'You're different, like me, Shane. Most guys would be groping me by now. But you're not.'

'Yeah!' was the only awkward thing I could reply to her.

Now if the truth be known, I was dying to kiss her, but I hadn't had any experience with women. I turned in upon myself after my mother died. While other guys were out gallivanting with girls, I stayed in my bedroom, listened to the radio, learnt chords and wrote. My social life consisted mostly of jamming and writing with my best friend Simon Langlands. If Julia thought I was good, wait until she copped a squiz at Simon. He could do every one of George Harrison's lead guitar licks. I went through the motions at school, never really participating in sport or the goss. Simon was the same. He was a newie that year. I felt sorry for the way he walked around the school all by himself on his first day. You see, my stupid friends thought it would be funny to ignore him. I went up to him, had a chat and discovered he played guitar. Of course those deadshits Evans, Sexton, Whitely and Adamson poofta-bashed him as well.

'Julia! Julia! Ocean child calls me, so I sing a song for love for Julia.' Jesus that's it! This wild ocean child's calling me; this Venus who's stepped out the ocean is calling me! From that night onwards, apart from Mary, there was room in my heart only for Julia. Our lives became one; I was to have another relationship, a marriage, but I loved only Julia.

She said I started snoring that night, so she replaced her lap with a pillow. The storm cleared by the time she got back to the village green. Julia and the Moonbirds danced the last decade away to an amazing Melbourne band, Spectrum. Julia told me she got shivers up and down her spine when a local piper came out onto the stage to do 'Auld Lang Syne'. Dad and Michael said the fireworks were fantastic after they found me on the couch snoring and dreaming. The story of my life!

2

Mother Nature

By the 1960s, despite its remoteness (Portmagee was perched on the most southern side of Australia) our old whaling town had a television in every house. Mary and I loved sitting on the couch together watching American family shows. All the young TV men had crew cuts and flashy white teeth, all the girls had pointed, covered breasts, ponytails and they dressed in long, flowing dresses or slacks. Well groomed Yankee mums and dads were repositories of wisdom, calm and neatness. Nobody lost their temper or displayed any passion; children ambled back from school through immaculately landscaped streets to their apron-wearing mothers waiting on the porch above a white picket fence. The TV mum cheerfully went about her domestic slavery while the pipe-smoking husband lounged in their favourite armchair or promenaded to and from work in cars the size of a fishing boat.

When I wasn't watching the idiot box, I played cowboys and Indians outside with my mates with silver six-shooters, or bought plastic World War II US marine helmets and big black machine guns, yelled out orders and felt inadequate because we didn't have strong accents like the Yanks.

My mother giggled at such a ridiculous notion and told me I had a beautiful voice. Like the television mothers, Mary was always there for me after school to give me dry biscuits with cheese and a cup of Milo. Unlike the American mothers, she'd easily shed a tear over some silly scene and often argued with my father, who ended up banishing himself to the garage out in our backyard. So much for father knows best.

American culture swept away our commonwealth of pink-coloured nations where the sun never sets. But with the assassination of the Kennedy brothers and Martin Luther King, those well-groomed American fathers of wisdom with big teeth, good men, were blown away by the gun. Loners destroy our better selves. Dreams are threatened by the forces of darkness. I remember Mary crying all night when she heard the Kennedy brothers were murdered.

My mother now lies with Granddad, Alan, and Gran, Loretta McNamara, in the Portmagee graveyard. My grandparents had an Irish lilt to their voices. Back in my childhood, you could go to some of the more remote towns of the Western District and still hear Irish accents, despite the speakers being fourth-generation Australian. One memory burnt into my childish mind was when that disgusting police chief of Saigon put a gun to the head of a suspected Vietcong guerilla and blew his brains out.

'Doesn't matter. He was only a commo!' my dad said.

'He may have been a commo, Jim, but he was still a human being,' replied my mother.

Bless you, Mother, with your bones resting below an extinct volcano and your blue eyes staring out upon the indifferent waters of Bass Strait.

There was that naked running Vietnamese girl, shrieking in sheer terror and agony, after her clothes and skin had been ripped off her by napalm! Every night, the family watched scenes of Americans bombing or shooting a Vietnamese village to pieces. The Statue of Liberty fell in the jungles of Indochina. Melbourne band the Skyhooks wrote a huge hit song about the news and called it 'Horror Movie'.

The radio with its uplifting music resonated upon our young ears and minds. It was a sanctuary from the violence, unlike the screen; it left room for the imagination. There was always a song with reassuring lyrics to shake you out of your teenage gloom, which reminded you

you were not alone and gave you strength to keep walking through a world where all the adult certainties were falling away.

Whenever I heard a stirring song, I always imagined I was a mean guitarist; my closest friends would materialise as the rest of the band. When my dad gave me a set of headphones, I'd blast my brains out in my bedroom living the rock 'n' roll dream. My love of music was in my blood; my mother was a professional singer but had to give it all away after she got married. I've got a record of her when she was seventeen winning the *Three Gong Award Show* on 3UZ. I still hear her sweet voice singing around the rooms of Wishart Street.

Mary was a walker and with my up-stretched hand in hers my boyish blue eyes took in the forever restless sky and ocean. I saw continents of cloud from Antarctica surge over our tiny town. I'd see rain shadows eventually produce gusts powerful enough to stop you walking. Mary and I often sought refuge from the rain below a Norfolk pine out on Griffith Isle; my head thawed upon her warm belly when she'd wrap my small body up in her coat. Swollen tides sometimes forced us off the sea wall; waves had 'your name written on them,' my mother chortled. Lightning exploded to rattle the whole township and cause blackouts. Within the jet-black darkness of the streets, she'd whisper, 'We're forced to think about things other than the trivial.' Rainbows dazzled the dunes and arced over the broiling ocean to declare a state of calm. Mum's smile was as large as the second rainbow.

In summer, the weather comes south from the desert to nudge the storms away. Portmagee would be blessed with powder-blue skies where Mary and I played in the shallows while my baby brother, Michael, slept below our beach umbrella. I noticed that unlike television mothers, Mary's breasts were round and bounced. You could see the veins in her thighs. I remember an old-timer always stood on top of the dunes to keep an eye out for sharks. But I was never afraid, because my mum was always there.

January was when the moonbirds hatched; my mother and I laughed at their cacophony at dusk. September brought the gales that carry the moonbirds back from the Aleutian Islands. Mary taught me they always return on the equinox and the whales appear at solstice.

I trudged for mile upon mile after her death, still feeling her hand in mine. One night, I took my tearful eyes off my boots and stared up into the sky where my mother shone like the evening star.

***

The spirit of the land never alters. It's silent, watching, absorbing, making allowances, giving guidance. Gods, thought to have been exterminated during the Tasmanian Black Wars, still impart their wisdom for those prepared to study them in the silent caves of the Grampians. The mountains speak to you at night. The Western District is blessed with hallowed grounds. Away from towns, people can sit and open their hearts to the hymn of winds and tide. Julia once showed me a sacred place in Yambuk where we found middens and evidence of ancient campfires. The chanting voices came to alter me.

The Western District's a vast flat tract of grassland, punctured by volcanoes that died not so long ago. These grasslands inspired the original European name 'Australia Felix'. The first custodians, the Gunditjmara, gave birth to these plains by firestick, creating rich hunting grounds; they used the volcanic rock to build houses and make eel traps around Lake Condah, which used to be a great gathering place for Aboriginal ceremony. Julia tells me she hears their corroborees sometimes when she slips in and out of her dreams.

One day, the Gunditjmara heard that the old man who held up the sky was in trouble. His props were under pressure and threatening to break. He needed more axes and rope to hold everything up. With great fear, the people arranged to send their tools and twine to the far side of the world. Then they spied the white sails dropping off gangs of white beings who began the great slaughter of seals, sea elephants and penguins. Some said the white spirits were their ancestors returned from the dead, others reckoned they must be devils because of the way they laughed at the wail of the defenceless creatures they bashed over the head with their clubs. Sometimes these white beings stole the women and killed their bravest with sticks of fire that made the sound of thunder. Death littered the beaches, then the sickness came and the old man finally fell out of the sky.

When the Irish came, they cleared the forests and built fences out of the volcanic rock. Their sheep runs were just like home. Indentured Catholics, survivors of the potato famine, slaved as tenant farmers, while their Protestant landlords lived the good life. They called their town Portmagee, their shire Belfast, their river Moyne. But the Gunditjmara had no concept of fixed boundaries and so fights broke out over access to the land and game. Seeing the whites had no compunction about killing kangaroos, birds, seals and whales, the Gunditjmara were perplexed when they were told they couldn't do the same to sheep and cows. Julia says a clan of the Gunditjmara were slaughtered by sealers near Portland when they tried to feast on a beached whale.

Julia's great-grandfather came from County Clare. His first language was Gaelic, his ancient Celtic beliefs thinly blanketed by Roman Catholicism and fuming under the yoke of Protestant oppression. While he was breaking his back constructing a stone fence, he shook his black curly head at the zealous Protestant government man who herded the Gunditjmara off to a mission. Then he heard a strange sound one Sunday as he walked along Killarney beach. He saw a brown body on the sand and assumed it was a seal. At first he thought the sound was wind whistling through the ribcage of a nearby slaughtered whale, but then Julia's ancestor realised he was listening to a dirge. The brown body wasn't some ocean animal resting from the strong sea currents. It was a woman, a naked woman tossed back onto the shore and left to die by the whalers. She became Julia's great-grandmother.

3

Off with the fairies

Bass Strait was calm the morning of my first hangover. Pea Soup Beach sighed like a sleeping dragon. The midday sun sometimes broke through my swaying curtain to burn my eyes and make my head feel as if was struck by an axe right in the middle. Little did I know then that this was to be a common result of mixing with Julia. In my coma, I thought I heard music drifting up from the Moyne River. Finally I dragged myself out of bed and staggered down the hallway in complete contrast to the previous night, going from immortal to near death in a matter of hours. I gave Mike his breakfast. My brother was in little boy television heaven; he'd spent all morning in *Cartoon Corner* and was looking forward to an afternoon of epic theatre. Dad snored like a trooper after his big night at the Caledonian.

After some cornflakes, a cuppa, and four Disprins, I stuck my head out of the front door, to discover the music I heard in my deathbed wasn't imagined. As the hemisphere of extreme pain moved from the top of my head to behind my eyes, the rhythm of the distant music echoed the calm tide of East Beach. Its far-away quality reminded me of the fairy stories Grandmother Loretta told me when I was a little boy. The good people lulled away villagers at night with a hypnotic music and they'd disappear forever into a fairy mound. Although, from what she told me, it wasn't a bad afterlife. The victim would spend an eternity dancing, singing, drinking, eating and generally cavorting with a pretty good-looking fairy queen. There's nothing wrong with any of that!

I followed the music through the avenue of giant Norfolk Island pines in Gipps Street. These trees always reminded me of a fleet of old sailing ships. A gold mountain range of cumulus cloud stretched high above Portmagee's glistening rooftops. The pain in my head started to lift. The music was coming from the old deserted flour mill. It was one of the town's original buildings, but Loretta reckons it had been deserted since the Great Depression after the poor owner, Ryan, hanged himself. It was double-storeyed like Seacombe Inn, but unlike the inn, the roof had fallen in and a huge oak tree grew out of the middle. I stuck my head through one of the open windows and saw Julia and her band practising in the shadows of the great tree. A crow in residence at the top of the oak groaned every time the Moonbirds hit a bum note; it groaned a lot.

A sunglasses-wearing Sue Sutcliffe was arguing with a sunglasses-wearing Julia King. With her unkempt thick red hair, red shirt and crimson jeans, Julia looked every inch the rock star.

'G'day, spunky trunks.' She lowered her sunglasses to the tip of her white pointed nose and gave me one of her devastating smiles.

'For God's sake, Julia, it's New Year's Day. All the sane people are resting! Why are we doing this nonsense! It's not as if we've got a gig coming up soon!' Sue's pixie face was flushed.

'Do you want to show them what you showed me last night?' Julia handed me her guitar as Steve snorted out a laugh.

'As the barmaid said to the bishop.' Steve cracked open a can of beer, then passed one to me.

I almost dropped Julia's guitar. 'Your guitar's strung for a right-hander, I'm left-handed.'

'Get your arse into gear, Macca. I'm a molly duke as well.' Alex Fitzsimmons pulled Julia's guitar off my chest and forced his upon me. 'Limp-wristed poof!'

'Fair suck of the sav!' Steve grinned at Alex then farted; his flatulence reminded me of the thunder that booms around Tower Hill.

All the Moonbirds laughed except for a disgusted Sue. I placed

Steve's can slowly on the ground then, nervously, slid Alex's strap over my shoulder and retuned his guitar. Steve shushed Alex when he blurted in disgust. Julia harmonised with me as I did a wonky version of the Everly Brothers' 'All I Have to do is Dream'. I picked up the can and gobbled down half its contents; another first for me, a beer in the middle of the day. A waning chalk moon lingered in the blue haze of the sky.

'See, what did I tell you guys? He's brilliant!' Beaming, Julia resumed her heated argument with Sue.

The drummer's black eyes rose to the clear sea sky when Alex joined in the debate.

Steve grabbed his six-pack then got up from his drums. 'Don't mind these tools, Macca. They're always going hammer and tongs. Some people call it creative tension but I call it bullshit. You're not a bad player for a carpet grub but you're dragging your heels.' Steve pointed his sausage finger at my half-drunk can.

The drummer was from the big smoke, Warrnambool. Although he was sixteen, he could get away with being twenty. Having long dark curly hair to his shoulders, thick black sidies, and pushing six foot, Steve was all muscle and rucked for Warrnambool. It was rumoured around the Western District that he was destined for the VFL; North Melbourne had sent out a couple of talent scouts. Being built like a brick shithouse meant that the drummer could stride into any bottle shop and pass as an eighteen-year-old. Thus he was the Moonbirds' prime source of alcohol. Standing in Steve's shadow, I felt I had no choice but to finish my beer.

'Here. Have another. It'll make a man out of you.' Steve handballed me a can. 'You look like you could do with it. Julia tells me you hit the grog last night. This is the best cure for the old hair of the dog.'

The solemn pledge I made to myself while vomiting in the early hours of the morning was thrown out the window. Steve was right: my headache and bottom of the cockie's cage mouth eased with each swig.

'You know, Macca, Julia's got big plans for us...' Steve stroked the black stubble on his chin. 'Portmagee, Warrnambool, Geelong, Melbourne then London. What do you reckon? I mean, I know we're as loose as a bride's nightie at the moment but...' Steve belched, 'I reckon we could give those useless Poms a run for their money. You could be our reserve in case anyone gets crook. All good teams have a strong reserve. What do you reckon, Macca? You don't say much for a little fella, do you?' Steve handballed Julia and Alex more cans of beer.

My mind reeled. London! London! The Mecca! The Holy Grail! The centre of the universe for every aspiring Aussie band. Steve's just offered me the position of backing guitarist for the Moonbirds! Me! Me! Bloody nonentity, insignificant me! In a handful of years, I could be in London, shoulder to shoulder with the Beatles, the Stones, the Who, Led bloody Zeppelin, Cream, Jimi Hendrix, the Small Faces... and that's just to name a bloody few of them. Me! A pimply, daggy, teenager from the arse end of the world! Mixing with the Gods! Is that why Julia visited me last night? Was she sussing me out?

'You know what shits me about the Poms is they're so up themselves. I meant look at all our grouse bands that have conquered Aus then dissolved in Pommy Land. The Twilights, the Master's Apprentices, Axiom...they're fucking snobs, the "bullet-headed Saxon mother's sons," to quote Johnnie Lennon.' Steve emptied his beer can. 'Hey, Julia. You got a spare fag for a dying Spartan?' He pulled a cigarette out of Julia's offered packet and lit it up. 'They still look down at us as bloody colonials.' White smoke bellowed out of his nostrils.

'The Easybeats made it.' Julia crushed her beer can, then opened another.

'Nah, Julia...it looks like they're going to be one-hit wonders.' Steve blew his smoke up into the blue sky.

'Ah well, all the more reason for us to bear the torch for our country, eh, fellas?' Julia replied.

'There's the Seekers,' Sue pointed out, before the rest of the Moonbirds tossed their beer cans at her.

I was peeved when I saw Julia put her arm around an upset Sue.

After some gentle coaxing, Sue began talking about her art. She was a prolific painter at St Theresa's Secondary and, unlike us, was being encouraged by her teachers to take up a scholarship. I'd seen some of her paintings in the Drill Hall at Banks Street. It was pretty good stuff,. She was madly into Salvador Dali. One painting that always stuck in my head was about the Black Thursday fires, the nightmarish bushfires which almost wiped out Portmagee a few years after settlement. Sue had placed a melting, crucified Christ in the middle of a fiery forest of giant matchsticks and cigarettes. Steve told me she was moody because she hated being taken away from her canvas. The Portmagee grapevine said she was a perfectly normal little girl until she fell of her horse and hit her head on a post. Whatever the cause, it was clear Julia held her under a spell.

'She's going to go far…whether she wants to take us along for the ride is another story. I really don't give a tinker's cuss, Macca. I've always got this as a fall back,' Steve held his beer can up to the smouldering January sun and laughed. 'Plus North Melbourne's putting out feelers.' (So the grapevine was true, I thought to myself.) Steve looked over to Julia. 'Oh yeah, she's gonna make it all right.'

The look of respect in this six-foot giant was something to behold. Julia and Sue were cracking jokes by now, their ridiculous banter soon infected the rest of the Moonbirds, and I hazily recall a terrific afternoon of us all stumbling around the dunes of Killarney Beach in search of the *Mahogany Ship*, a fabled Portuguese caravel that was shipwrecked here in the fifteenth century. A hysterical Steve kept tugging planks out of the sand then held them up to us as proof.

4

Eye of the storm

Dad's favourite watering hole, the Caledonian, has a plaque out the front claiming that it's Victoria's oldest licensed pub. The locals call it the Stump because the second storey was never finished; dormer windows stick out of the iron corrugated roof, but the pub's attic rooms were abandoned when the labourers downed tools and headed off for the Ballarat goldfields. The Stump's had live music for as long as anyone can remember. Dad's band Captain Starlight, had been playing there for donkeys. The author of *Robbery Under Arms*, Rolf Boldrewood, used to sell his horses out in the Stump's yard. With its low ceilings, pine doors, hand-adzed hallway timber and regular pisspots, it's quite a place, and prone to getting rowdy sometimes.

It was here the Moonbirds first performed. Dad arranged it; he was a drinking mate of the Stump's publican, Bernie Mullens. While I was snoring on New Year's Eve, Dad had a liquid conversation with Bernie and talked him into me being the support act of Captain Starlight. After my dad saw how nervous I was, he agreed that I should have some of my friends on the stage with me. When I approached Julia and Simon, Julia jumped at the chance but Simon had to be dragged kicking and screaming. It wasn't exactly my first performance; whenever the McCarthys got together, we'd always have a family singalong. Granddad Alan would do a few tunes on his mouth organ; he once had his own harmonica band that toured all of Victoria. Mother Mary's angelic voice always brought a tear to my infant eye when she'd do a love ballad. Dad would sing a few folk songs at the piano, I'd do my fifties stuff on guitar and young Mikey would sing something more contemporary like the Monkees. Sometimes Mary and I would be called up on stage at the Stump to perform with Captain Starlight, so entertaining wasn't foreign to me. But nothing prepared me for my first stage appearance with the Moonbirds.

Julia and I decided to rehearse in my bathroom in Wishart Street because it had good acoustics. Julia, Simon and I had to stand in the bath so Steve could squeeze in with his drum kit in, Sue couldn't make it because of her painting; Alex refused to join us because he didn't want to perform with 'a pack of pimply little deadshits'.

Julia smiled at Simon as he mumbled to himself sitting on the bath's ledge to retune his guitar. 'Shane tells me you can do "Here Comes the Sun".'

'C'mon, Moonface, give it a whirl! I'm building up a thirst here.' Steve tested his cymbals, belched, then pulled a beer out of his aran jumper.

Red flushes splattered across Simon's round cheeks.

'C'mon, Simon, I've been praising you to the hilt. Show them what you're made of.' When I ruffled my mate's thick dark-brown curly hair, he sniffed, hesitated, then broke into the opening chords. They were perfect.

Julia sang and we all joined in on the chorus, 'Sun! Sun! Sun! Here we come!'

I threw on my guitar then time stood still in an afternoon of jamming.

Russell Ives was ringleader of the Stump's pisspots; he'd turned into an alcoholic after being thrown out of Portmagee High for being a bully of a teacher. Unfortunately for Julia, he tended to blame her for his downfall; within a matter of months he'd gone from a slim, arrogant, dark-haired and bearded know-it-all, to a fat grey-haired, bushy-bearded arrogant, drunken know-it-all. He gestured lewdly at Julia as the Moonbirds set up their instruments. Usually her foul look would put him back in his box, but his pisspot mates kept egging him on.

Bernie Mullens's blue eyes twinkled below his silver bushy eyebrows. The local pisspots always behaved like this to women, the publican thought to himself; the opposite sex had no right to be in the bar, plus Russell and his mates were always a reliable source of money.

Julia's mother and aunts arrived to sip shandies in the Ladies' Lounge. Julia's mother, Eve, with her thickly sprayed gold beehive hair, fox coat dangling across her shoulders, lemon-coloured dress and bulging white handbag, was the eldest sister of the six Douglas girls. All the Douglases had the chiselled features of the stone idols of Easter Island. The story had it that they inherited these features from their great-grandmother, the original Eve.

The original Eve was a young Scottish migrant on the clipper ship *Loch Derg*, which smashed into Mutton Bird Island in June 1878. There were fifty-four passengers and crew aboard, Eve was washed into a gorge and pulled ashore by a fifteen-year-old apprentice, Tom Bryce. The two ended up being the only survivors. Tom left her on top of a cliff then found some shepherds who raised the alarm. Her face was set like a rock when she was rescued late next morning. Eve was only sixteen when she lost her parents and six siblings. It was this identical look that Julia gave Russell.

We wiped the vomit from our chins after Julia dragged Simon and me from the bathroom basin. Then, as we crawled onstage, Russell started abusing us, but our lead singer defied him with her burning red hair and low-cut short black dress.

'The last time I saw a mouth like that it had a hook in it!' Julia leered as the rest of the pisspots roared with laugher. 'C'mon, boys, let's stick it up them! "Get Back"!'

Julia snarled at Russell, Simon strummed his guitar, Steve took a swig of a beer then pounded away, I followed Simon's lead and the Moonbirds spluttered into life. We were flat as a tack at first, but people kept trickling through the Stump's ancient front door and smiled at us before they bought a drink. We played loud and non-stop, all of us hoping that our music would shut stupid Russell and his pisspots up. It didn't work and more of the regulars (fishermen and labourers) started to jeer at us.

Then when my beaming dad walked through the front door holding Michael's hand, his face transformed into bewilderment. 'Hey, guys, watch your language! Set an example – there's kids in the bar!'

'They fucking shouldn't be here. This is a man's fucking place not a place for fucking billy lids,' Russell eyeballed my father, 'or fucking gins or long-haired pooftas!'

'Right, that's it!' Steve tossed his drumsticks down, plucked his beer bottle off the stage and smashed it over Russell's head.

The drunkard collapsed like a slaughtered cow.

'Any of you other wrinkly arseholes want to have a go?' Steve loomed over the stage like an angry leviathan. 'Nah? It's always been my theory that the louder the mouth, the smaller the dick. C'mon, Jules, let's show these dribble-dicks.' The drummer dropped his bottle neck then stared at Julia who was as rigid as a statue. 'C'mon, Jules, it's rumoured in our family that we've got blackfella in us too. If you scratch the surface of everyone in this God-forsaken country, you'd probably find more blackfellas than anyone wants to admit. C'mon, Jules, you should be proud.'

Julia shuddered as Simon strummed the first few notes of 'While My Guitar Gently Weeps'. The proprietor dragged the bloated unconscious body from the dance floor. Julia gradually smiled as my younger brother danced and applauded the band.

An old rocker came through the front door. He turned out to be Julia's father, Freddie King. He started dancing with Mikey. The rest of the Moonbirds family arrived – Steve's whopping Warrnambool footy mates turned up and before we knew it, a dancing, appreciative, audience materialised in front of us. Russell's beer-sodden mob held up the bar. the Moonbirds entered into a musical trance; we became the eye of the storm. I can still picture Julia's liquid, sparkly eyes, her black-stocking legs almost kicking over her shoulders, and Steve's big chin sticking defiantly out at the crowd, Simon happily, Chuck Berry-like hunching over a riff and me snorting laughs back to my band mates. We were immortal!

Sue had her arm around Julia later on that night as we walked along the seawall to the lighthouse. A full moon poked in and out of a procession of racing clouds. When the moon was out, she transformed the sea into a lapping silver lake of lace. You could see all the way out to the flat limestone island the Gunditjmara called Deen Maar, the isle of the dead. When the moon went in, vast shadowed spirits stalked the dunes and the waves turned into maddened snakes. An occasional mutton bird gargled out a protest against Steve's loud laughter or the clank of a beer can. Julia and Sue smoked and whispered to each other in front of us.

'Don't worry about her, guys.' Steve chuckled at the hunched shadow behind us. It was Simon, still under the deluded belief he was too young for our company. 'That arsehole Ives spooked her a bit. You see, he put the big word on Julia. He thought her constant shit stirring meant she had the horn for him, but she gave him a hard time because he was a bloody oaf. Plus, she's shocked at seeing Freddie. See, he's more like a ghost than a bloody father. He's a merchant seaman. Julia's the daughter of a sailor. Here you go, young fellas.' Steve hauled the beer slab off his shoulder and handballed Simon and me a beer. 'He's never around, he can't stand Eve, he's a prick! You see, he stole Julia from Eve when she was five and took her away to Warrnambool for a weekend. He spoilt her, took her to the movies, the sea carnival and stuff, then Eve found out what hotel they were staying in and demanded Julia back. Freddie told Julia she had to make up her mind who she'd prefer to live with. When poor Julia chose Freddie, Eve stormed off with a crying Julia chasing after her screaming, "Mumma, don't go! Daddy, come home!" Prick! A kid shouldn't have to be put through that garbage. Freddie's still doing it now. He disappears for years then suddenly rocks up to play all sorts of mind games with her. He still fucking hasn't grown up. I mean, it's 1970 and he's still pretending to be a rocker! What a drag!'

Across the ocean, the gold lights of Warrnambool glowed as we sat below the lighthouse. Its beam swept across Bass Strait to ignite the homeward paths of time. My mind was like a roller-coaster. Julia! I wanted to comfort her but…she seemed to be in good hands. After an eternity, she raised her head to slowly reveal a smile. Sue grinned as well; they looked like two imps below the moon. A planet peeped out of the clouds.

'That's it, Julia! To quote Jimi Hendrix, "There are many here among us who feel that life is but a joke!"' Steve handballed two beers to the giggling girls then danced as he sang 'All Along the Watchtower'.

Thank God for our drummer, his beer and his wisdom. the Moonbirds drank, smoked, laughed, bullshitted then became a band of careless silver spirits below a full moon, trodden on only six months before by Neil Armstrong. We were on the cusp of a new age. For the first time, we saw our planet dangle like a blue jewel in the vastness of space. It meant something to have long hair and question our parents' values. Something was brewing worldwide and we Moonbirds, perched on the edge of Bass Strait, sensed we were to be a part of it. Warrnambool's bright lights beckoned. Steve's footy mates loved the band and wanted us to play at the footy club's functions. I suppose you love any form of music when you're totally pissed.

5

Hell to heaven

I was being snarled at again. I knew the mouth well. There was a gaping hole in the front because its owner decided to blow on grog the money his parents had given him to fix his teeth. The gap occurred during a stolen car crash. The yellow teeth were well lubricated with spit. I'd wiped sticky globs of this muck off my faces several times. Grimacing Paul Evans, his mates Heath Sexton, Neville Whitely and Leigh Adamson bailed me up behind the deserted Customs House beside the river. I'd decided to go for a morning walk along the jetty before Simon came over. We'd planned to write some songs together. As Mary taught me, a walk's always good for inspiration and dissolving any melancholy that might be lingering in your bedroom.

Paul 'Ebbo' Evans clenched his fists then circled me like a hornet. He grimaced, snorted then spat a ball of snot straight into my eyes. His three companions cacked themselves silly. I couldn't see, so I raised both of my hands in a gesture of surrender. Ebbo punched me several times in the face. I reeled away, but luckily this time I wasn't going to be 'poofta bashed'. Simon's mum, Anne, raced up to us. Ebbo and gang took off as soon as they saw her. I staggered back up and tried to wipe away my tears as she came up to me.

'You all right, Shane?' Anne stroked my forehead and examined my cheek. 'You poor thing. I'm going to talk to that slack father of yours. He's got to do something about those barbarians.'

'I'm all right, Mrs Langlands. Really I am.'

'Rubbish you are. It's that sort of macho nonsense that allows those swine to get away with murder.' Anne steamed through her thick black-rimmed glasses; it was the look that always coerced her students at St. Theresa's Secondary into quick submission. She took out her hanky, wetted it with her tongue and started to rub my cheek. 'Where's your father?'

'In bed.'

'Typical! You tell him when Simon comes over I'm coming with him to talk about those bullies! Their savagery can't go on. Go home now, love.' She gave me a hug then gently turned me towards Wishart Street.

I walked home rubbing my stinging cheekbone. My stomach was in a knot, mainly because no one had spoken to me like that since my mum passed away. I sneaked into the back door and stared through my red eyes in the bathroom mirror to see that a black egg had sprouted from the side of my face. I placed a flannel under the cold water tap and gasped when I applied it to the bruise. I fell onto my bed. Midge jumped onto my lap and as I scratched her ears, the combination of her lawnmower purr and warm January sunlight streaming through my window lulled me off to sleep. I dreamt Julia and I were eagles, slowly circling each other, miles up in the sky.

I woke up to the sound of Anne's angry voice and my dad's laughter.

When Simon slunk into my bedroom, his jaw looked like a steel letterbox. 'Jesus, Shane, you look like you've been hit by a bus! Do you want to forget about writing this arvo?' My friend stroked his pimply chin then rubbed me on the shoulder.

'Nup. One thing Mary told me before she passed away is that you've got to keep getting on with life.' I leant over, picked my exercise book from under the bed and with a pounding heart showed Simon my lyrics.

My mate took a long time to read them. Then he placed my book in the middle of the bed, sat down with his guitar, stared at my words and hummed then strummed. I did the same. Sometimes we eyeballed each other and as the East Beach whispered, our parents fought. Simon and I started to compose our own music.

Later on that evening, we laughed while we piffed yonnies across the water; we were silent when the bloated sun lunged like an angry god into the red wine ocean. Songs brewed behind our glowing red faces.

6

Flaming troublemaker

I was in the newsagency after school looking at some World War II magazines when I saw Julia striding down Sackville with a big smile on her face. She met Sue out the front of Belfast Bakery, then giggled as they sat down for a milk shake and muffins. I was dying to know what she was so happy about. Julia and Sue raised their faces to the February sky and with their half-opened eyes they reminded me of the way my cats daydream in the sun.

I bought a magazine about Kokoda and decided to go to the milk bar for a pint of strawberry milk. Swallows swooped down from their nests in the shop veranda beams above me. I stepped into the shop and had a bit of a yarn with the owner Mr Byrne as he put some flavouring into my milk bottle and stirred it.

'Hmph…' he snorted through the grey bristles of his moustache and pointed his pink nose across towards the bakery, 'that one's up to no good again. The sooner she has a baby and settles down the better, flaming troublemaker! Here you go young fella, that's a zac, thanks.' Mr Byrne held out his shaky palm to take my five cents. His big belly shook like jelly at the sight of Ebbo and his mates coming through the rainbow-coloured plastic strips dangling at the entrance to his shop. 'G'day, dig, how's it going? You up to no good, eh?'

The older residents of Portmagee called Ebbo 'dig' because his angry, alcoholic father had fought in New Guinea during the war. How the old codgers of the town managed to tarnish the noble tradition of the digger with the Evans men was beyond me.

'G'day, you old bastard. Hello, poof!' Ebbo turned his white curly head towards me as Mr Byrne chuckled.

I ignored the dropkick and stepped out into Sackville Street.

'Shane!' Julia jumped out of her chair and gestured for me to join them.

I crinkled my eyes as I made my way across the glare of the hot asphalt street. Why the powers-that-be decided to start school during the height of summer when the kids are too hot to learn never made any sense to me. The only concession the Education Department made to the stinking heat is that we could take our ties off when it was a hundred degrees. Whoopty bloody do!

'How was your first day back?'

As Julia pointed me to a chair, I couldn't help but notice the low cut in her crimson T-shirt.

'Bloody boring, as usual.' I slurped my straw. 'How was yours?'

'Wonderful, Shaney, wonderful. I'm starting the year off with a bang!' Her eyes glistened like the waves below a full moon.

'What do you mean?' My slurps got louder as I reached the bottom of the bottle.

'I've been expelled! Hallelujah! There's a god after all!' Julia held her arms up to the smouldering sun.

'You wha'!' The straw dropped out of my mouth.

'Expelled, kicked out, nicky wooped, given short shrift, pea sauced, given the boot, given the arse. It's bloody wonderful.' Julia lit a cigarette.

'What the bloody hell happened, Julia? What did you bloody do, you wacker?'

'It was a classic, Shaney. Me and Alex went down to the smoking tree during afternoon recess. Christ, it had been a long day! Anyway, Alex produces this joint. We were having a few tokes when we got sprung bad by Mr Davidson. God, I hate that prick, the way he bangs on about the war and what a good job our blokes are doing. I had a stoush with him, telling him if he's so enthusiastic why doesn't he bloody well go and fight? Anyway, the arsehole snuck up to me and

Alex, then orders us into the principal's office. By that time, we've got the giggles. Well, that's the worst way to behave in front of those fascists, isn't it! Have you noticed fascists have no sense of humour? Imagine if stand-up comics had been allowed to flourish in Berlin? Hitler was such a sitting duck with his square moustache and huge knickerbockers. So old Thomas expels us, tells us he's going to contact our parents, the usual palaver. As if my parents will give a rats. My old man's never around and me Ma's always working. By this time, Alex's wetting his pants. It was a hoot, I tell you!' Julia laughed so much she started coughing.

'You silly sausage, Julia. How far do you think you're going to get in the crazy world without an education?'

Sue shook her head and flicked crumbs down to some busy, chirping sparrows.

'With the Moonbirds, we're going to the toppermost of the poppermost, right, Shane?'

'Um yeah, I guess so!'

'What do you mean you guess so? I fucking know so, Shane! We're gonna make it big, I feel it in my bones!'

'Oh no!' Sue groaned at the sight of Alex Fitzsimmons walking towards us with a grin as wide as Sackville Street.

Somehow Sue and I got roped into hitch-hiking with them to Tower Hill to smoke some more dope. I was nervous as I sat on the back of the ute taking us up to Tower Hill. I'd never touched the stuff before, but being sixteen you're compelled to act as a veteran when it comes to things like sex and drugs. The irony is that the people you're trying to impress usually know that you're talking bullshit anyway and that you're barely a babe out of the woods.

And into the woods we went, into this State Reserve between Portmagee and Warrnambool. It's about as remote as you can get. Tower Hill's an old volcano that last erupted only seven thousand years ago. The crater's now a huge blue lake surrounded by miles and miles of bush and full of wildlife. At dusk, heaps of kangaroos come out of the park to graze in the nearby paddocks. Every time Mike and I go for a walk around the lake, we have koala-counting competitions; our last count was twenty-five. Emus like to check you out to see if you've got any good tucker. I thought of the tiger snakes that love to sun themselves on the rocks as Julia found us an isolated outcrop where you could see all the way back to Portmagee.

'The secret to a good innocent fellow,' (Julia's nickname for a joint), 'Shaney, is to drag it right into your lungs like this.' She smoked and breathed deeply. 'Ah, the sweet smell of success.' She smiled like the Cheshire cat as she handed me the joint.

I puffed then tentatively drew the smoke deep into my stomach. Nothing happened at first; I just lay back on my elbows and studied the Portmagee peninsula sticking out like a gold arm into Bass Strait. A toadstool cloud fled towards Warrnambool.

'Don't you care about what happened today, Julia?' Sue took the smoke from my fingers and took a drag.

'In the words of Henry Lawson, "I'm past caring", Sue. Now stop gasbagging and hand it around, will you?' Julia pointed towards me.

I took a few more tokes then slowly became aware of every wave that formed on the horizon. I marvelled as they transformed from a long line into a stretching silver serpent which glided to the nearby shore of Killarney Beach. The tide sang like a sea shanty. Seabirds performed a shoreline ballet as they glided along the waves. The harsh sun became an embracing goddess.

Then I heard the voice of an angel. It was Julia singing the traditional ballads of our grandmothers. I somehow found my head in Sue's lap as she harmonised with Julia and stroked my hair. Alex was silent. The only thing I heard from him was the occasional laugh. Every nerve in my body tingled with joy. A cricket orchestra chirped away nearby. My spirit floated off to Deen Maar; I was convinced I was in an Arthurian dream sailing off to the isle of Avalon.

I don't recall how I got home, all I remember is muttering something to my dad about being tired and going straight to bed, where I masturbated for hours; each orgasm felt like it went for an eternity. I kept picturing Julia's chest below her crimson T-shirt.

Alex was sacked from the Moonbirds that night; he and Julia were having a great time taking potshots at sheep, but she exploded when he killed a kangaroo. In Julia's eyes, European animals were vermin, native animals sacred.

I wrote reams of poetry, convinced I was Australia's answer to Shakespeare. Next morning I woke up a little bit cloudy-headed and sore, yet looking forward to reading the most profound words ever to come out of this country, but soon discovered I'd produced complete self-indulgent crap.

7

Guiding lights

During Freddie's last trip to Melbourne, he got a peace badge for his daughter from some waterside union drinking mates. Julia wore it with pride. When she came back from her suspension, Mr Davidson and the more conservative teachers of Portmagee High were outraged. The principal, Mr Thomas, ordered her to take it off; Julia refused and was suspended again.

When she wore the badge on stage during a Moonbirds performance at the Warrnambool Footy Club, a few dropkicks gave her a hard time until Steve yelled at them to shut up.

Sometimes we played in the old dance hall on the outskirts of Portmagee. It's a decaying wooden structure built at the turn of the last century on the site of the first Catholic church. You go through an avenue of red gums to get there. Granddad Alan told me his grandfather, Brendan, together with the first Irish settlers, used to sing in Gaelic during the service, something they weren't allowed to do back home. The church burnt down in the 1890s. Some say it was lit deliberately by some Presbyterians who couldn't stand the 'satanic' sound of the hymns; others reckon the priest, Father Milligan, had a big session at the Stump and fell asleep during his last pipe for the night.

'Squid' Murray, a cray fisherman, played piano accordion at the hall; 'The Ghost', Brian Jones, a baker from the Belfast Bakery, played the fiddle; and sometimes they were accompanied on vocals by Kitty Moore, a Koroit beauty with pointed features and long gold hair. They played folk tunes for over a decade. Alan's father, Miley, used to join in on the circle dancing as a young boy. The music stopped abruptly in 1918 when Kitty lost her brother in the battle of Mont St Quentin. The music of Squid, the Ghost and Kitty lives on, though; the locals reckon you can hear their songs in the canopies of the avenue of red gums on a windy night. My Da remembers old Miley used to sing these tunes at our family dos right up until he died. Captain Starlight continues to play them to this very day.

Family ghosts always joined me whenever the Moonbirds played at the old dance hall. Dark-bearded Brendan sat in the front row singing the ancient language of our people, Miley dancing as a boy, Alan, spruced up in his suit and tie played his harmonica with me on stage, Mary, with her long flowing checkered dress and sunset-coloured top, danced in the middle of the hall. Our tiny, dusty, ember of hall light glowed in the Western District's ocean of darkness and smiled at her sisters the stars.

The Moonbirds started to get a reputation around the traps; before we knew, it we had a gang of groupies. Steve was over the moon and usually disappeared with an army of young women after each gig. Julia kept her male fans at an arm's distance and spent her free time with Sue, where they drank, smoked and discussed how they could oppose the Vietnam War, or they argued over Sue staying in the band.

Simon and I were all at sea, neither of us used to girls making it obvious that they only wanted us for our weedy bodies. One night we succumbed to two groupies, Helen Barker and her friend Lynette Johnson. They were both sophisticated girls from the big smoke, Warrnambool. Helen had thick curly blonde hair and modelled her appearance on Bette Midler; Lynette was dark, long, lean and was a dead ringer for Cher Bono. Lynette's nickname was 'the gypsy' because of her dark features and the fact that she lived in a caravan in her parent's backyard. Some Portmagee residents believed Lynette's dark features were due to having an Abo in the family somewhere, but the Johnsons were disgusted at the thought. Lynne's father said her features came from Spanish sailors washed ashore in Ireland after the Armada came to grief.

The girls persuaded us to go back to Lynette's place because her parents had gone away for the weekend. Simon and I were a bit knackered after playing for three hours straight. We stuck our young fingers out on the Princes Highway. Satellites glided across the Milky Way's luminous backbone as we giggled under the influence of a bottle of white wine. Heat lightning flickered over Bass Strait. A cocky from Koroit gave us a lift to Warrnambool. Lynette pulled another bottle of plonk out of her parent's fridge; Helen produced a matchbox of dope. The girls laughed hysterically when we told them we called joints 'innocent fellows'.

In a glazed alcoholic state, I admired the way Helen was a master of the art of rolling a reefer. Lynette dimmed the lights and put on some Jimi Hendrix. I lay down on the floor, closed my eyes and was transported straight to Woodstock. Helen lay down next to me, took a toke of the joint then kissed and blew the smoke into my mouth. I left Woodstock for the edge of the universe. Before I knew it, she had unzipped my fly.

One trait I had with smoking dope was that if there was any music around I became totally one with it. Nothing could distract me. I worshipped at the altar of God, who at that time was Jimi Hendrix. I marvelled over the sonic poetry of his guitar work. Simon told me later on that he was in the same 'cosmic dimension'. Helen whispered into my ear that we should go out to the caravan. Genuinely disappointed, because I wanted to keep experiencing Jimi, I delayed things for a bit by telling Helen I wanted to have a cigarette first.

Lynette went into the kitchen to make a cup of tea. When I asked a recumbent Simon for the matches, he didn't seem to hear me. The matches were on a stool directly in front of him.

'Simon, could you pass us the matches, thanks?' I groaned as I leant up from the floor. It seemed to take an eternity to rise. 'Simon, could you pass us the matches?' I stared at my friend; his eyes were closed and he looked like he'd been hit by a truck. 'Simon!' I shouted this time. 'Could you pass me the flaming matches!'

'I don't know if I can do that, Shane.'

'What do you mean, you don't know if you can do it!'

'I'm pretty stoned at the moment and what you're asking me is really complicated.'

Helen took my hand and led me out to the caravan. We smoked some more dope and when I waffled on about God knows what she placed a finger to my lips then kissed me again. She lit a candle and took me to the caravan bed. I watched in deep admiration as she took her clothes off. She started to take my T-shirt off then nudged me onto the bed. I'd read in a women's magazine that the way to get a woman aroused was to circle her nipple with your tongue. Helen purred like a cat and sat on top of me.

Unfortunately nothing happened that night. The same thing happened to Simon with Lynette. And so, from sheer cowardice, Simon and I refused to mingle with the groupies after our show. We developed a reputation for being cool and aloof towards women, though some thought because Simon and I were so close, we must be gay. The truth was we were two shit-scared virgins.

The consequence was, however, that Simon and I managed to get closer to Julia and Sue.

Sometimes Julia came over to Sackville Street to join in our songwriting. Her ideas were invaluable; she emphasised the female side in our love songs and she also told us we should start writing about our land, both pretty radical ideas in the early 1970s. Love songs back then tended to be gooey or male-centred, plus hardly any songs ever included references to Australia. American and British rock 'n' roll dominated the airwaves, Aussie bands sang about Arkansas Grass or St Louis.

Simon and I started composing songs about Portmagee, The Great Ocean Road, Tower Hill, Warrnambool, even Geelong. Julia had a magnificent bullshit detector when it came to our words too. We'd write about life getting better and she'd throw in stuff about things getting worse. Considering our shared Celtic heritage, she suggested we include some traditional rhythms in our songs. But she said, we should always keep our songs punchy and not get into the flower-power rubbish that seemed to be everywhere at that moment. Steve told the guerillas in the audience to shut up again when the Moonbirds started to play more of their original songs rather than old standards. Our unique music would have died at birth if not for our big, burly drummer.

Sue encouraged Simon and me to continue taking Art and Literature as subjects at Portmagee High. She introduced us to the wonderful worlds of the Renaissance, the Impressionists and the Surrealists. By knowing in intimate detail the lives of the great painters, novelists and poets, she gave us a richer perspective on things. I'll never forget the arguments she gave in defence of Shakespeare. She told us not to listen to the ridiculous bullshit often used to put down old Will. Ignoramuses used to state that nobody ever spoke like that back then. Of course they didn't, Sue argued. Shakespeare wrote poetry. If you just shut up and listen to his words, even close your eyes, you'd discover the beauty of his language. He wasn't a high flatulent Pommie snob, but like your average Aussie he loved his beer and a good yarn.

I remember when I turned sixteen I made a conscious decision to answer questions put to the class by the teachers and engage them in discussion. I know others in my class thought I was a smart arse, but I didn't care any more. Thanks to the female Moonbirds, a whole new world of knowledge opened up for Simon and me.

8

Adventures with Freddie

Freddie King was back in town, renting a house in Albert Street, which was handy for the Moonbirds because it was only a stone's throw from the dance hall. Freddie told his daughter that his house was always open to her and her friends. As a result Julia, Simon and I often visited him. When Eve banged on the front door, demanding that her daughter come home, Freddie smiled and ignored her. The other Moonbirds stayed away. It was winter and Sue spent most of her waking hours in her parents' attic in Grant Street painting. With the roaring wind and constant heavy rain, it was a good time to be indoors and create. Steve kept away, claiming Warrnambool was playing good footy and looked like being in the finals for the first time in donkey's years.

We partied a lot in Albert Street. Freddie's fridge was always well stocked. Julia's Da entertained us with his sailing stories. He was in the British Merchant Navy up to and during World War II. On one occasion, he'd been bashed in a jail in Rio de Janeiro after a drunken brawl with some German sailors.

'The bastards tried to argue there was no difference in the way we both obeyed orders from above. I told them there was a huge difference between obeying orders from an elected prime minister compared with a sewer rat like Hitler,' Freddie said with a gleam in his eye. Although blue, it was the same gleam as his daughter's. His frequent cheeky look was also identical to Julia's. He told us he'd been stalked by German bombers, witnessed a nearby tanker snap in two after it had been hit by a U-boat in the Atlantic and sailed through the Arctic Circle all the way to Murmansk.

'Did you learn anything while you were in the navy?' Simon sipped his beer.

'What did I learn? Hmm…' Freddie dropped his large red-coloured head back and took a deep draw of his cigarette. 'Sean Connery was a drinking mate of mine and when he was asked the same question he said, "I learnt that there was an arsehole above me, an arsehole above him and an arsehole above him and that basically I was answerable to a chain of arseholes." I couldn't get out quick enough. Rules are made to be broken, kids. The shit floats to the top.' Freddie gave a long sigh.

Julia's father played banjo and it was he who had taught Julia her first chords when she was a little girl. Sometimes he joined in on our jam sessions. Instead of a tiny bathroom, we now had a huge back room in Albert Street for practice. Freddie was a great player; Simon and I listened to him carefully. Until then, we tended to think the banjo was a bit of a daggy old-fashioned instrument, but hearing him weaving his melodies through ours changed our minds. It had a magic all of its own; you could hear hundreds of years of suffering and joy bursting from Freddie's fingers.

Despite his childhood neglect of Julia, she adored him. He was more like a friend than a father. He idolised his daughter and her dreams. I'd never met an adult like him. Not once did he lay down the law; he was always sunny and he spoke to us like we were his equals. It was wonderful being in a home that didn't have any rules. He didn't care if he let the house and garden go to rack and ruin.

We discovered Freddie had a network of drinking contacts all over Australia, if not the world. One of his mates was Gary Kelly in Geelong, who owned a record studio and promoted Aussie acts. He was trying to resurrect the career of his brother Johnnie. Johnnie was huge in Australia in the 1950s and early 60s. He even got to America, but his raw brand of rock 'n' roll didn't go over well. The country was going through that boring stage of music before the Beatles where they loved schmaltzy teen ballads and every singer was named either Bobbie or Frankie. After dominating the Australian market, poor old Johnnie realised he had nowhere else to go and he sank into a depressive, alcoholic stupor for a decade. Gary was trying to give him a focus by getting him back into the studio. Trouble was, Gary told Freddie one night in Geelong's Scottish Chief's Hotel, neither brother had enough money to hire a professional band. Freddie's eyes lit up and before we knew it we were in the back of a Bedford van on the road to Geelong.

I had a knot in my stomach all the way along the Princes Highway, I think we all did. A series of storms hit us; Julia chained-smoked and chatted incessantly with Freddie in the front seat as he peered through the swishing windscreen wipers. When Steve fed cans of beer over the front seat, he reminded me of those old World War II newsreels of American soldiers hurling grenades at the enemy. Silent Simon kept rubbing the condensation off the back window with his sleeve. Freddie's driving skills were amazing; he flew along a road which had long disappeared into a thick cloud of silver. Thank God for Steve being his normal, chatty self; he once more managed to drag me out of my teenage fear of a challenge.

Johnnie Kelly was a legend; he managed to loosen up the Moonbirds with some more beer and we somehow managed to back him up on his new single, 'She's My Lady'. After that, Johnnie took us back to his favourite watering hole, the Grand Hotel at Portarlington, where Freddie shouted us all a counter meal. We had a fantastic afternoon.

Johnnie, dressed immaculately in a white suit and tie, regaled all the patrons with stories, songs and wise advice. I remember nodding to his gold-ringed fingers, but unfortunately can't recall any of his words because I was so snakes-hissed! What I do remember from that long afternoon was that the clouds lifted for a second and I got my first glimpse of Port Phillip Bay. I swore I saw all the way across that vast flat expanse of water to Melbourne's grey beckoning towers. We froze to death as Freddie drove us back home that night; we were so cold, in fact, that I ended up being in the middle of a human sandwich. I collapsed on top of Steve as he snored on the van floor and Simon fell on top of me. Julia said we slept like that all the way home to Portmagee.

9

Richard Barton goes west

Richard Barton suffered from a nasty hangover. God, how he hated work! He'd been raging in Melbourne all weekend, but it was now six-thirty Monday morning in Geelong. His spirit felt as barren as the volcanic plains surrounding his home town. He was the owner of Dick's Goods, a new white goods store given to him as an eighteenth birthday present by his parents. They thought the name was hilarious, Richard hated it. When he tried to suggest something more contemporary, like Cool for Cats (reference to the store's vast number of fridges and the local footy team), his parents thought it sounded too hippie. As his father said to him, the Bartons had been in white goods since Adam played full back for Jerusalem and weren't about to change now. From the moment he could talk, Richard was groomed to become the future head of the Bartons' Geelong financial empire. Trouble was, he was hopeless with money.

He stared at his alarm clock. It was now pushing seven. As the young man rubbed his large Celtic brow, pain stretched all the way from his blue eyes, across the top of his red-headed scalp to the back of his skull. He slid his thin naked body out of bed and the pain intensified as he crawled across the floor for some Disprin. Fuck it! He wasn't going in today. The bloody assistant manager, Keith Gould, a hard-drinking bald Welshman, could look after Dick's Goods today while Richard worshipped at the porcelain altar.

Richard vanished into Melbourne every chance he had. The city teemed with new and exciting music. He discovered a number of hangouts where he could catch a band, drink and dance the night away with spunky women. The Much More Ballroom, Kew Club, the Box Hill Town Hall – they were all jammed packed with teenagers eager to get as drunk as a skunk and forget about the boring weekly grind of work. Fantastic live bands blossomed everywhere. Daddy Cool played a mean brand of 50s rock. Chain and Carson slew the audience with their raunchy style of blues. Billy Thorpe and the Aztecs blew the roof off every venue they played. Axiom amazed the crowd with their thumping rhythm section. The Masters Apprentices varied their mix with powerful hard rock and heart-wrenching ballads. Russell Morris was always guaranteed to get everyone up on the dance floor. Spectrum bemused the crowd with their quirky songs. And grinning Richard was always there, right in the middle of the crowd, stomping and shaking muscles nobody thought could be shaken. Some said he danced like he'd just sat on a nest of bull ants; others said his style was more akin to a nutcase putting out a grass fire.

Some of these musicians grew up in migrant hostels, where they shared their love of rhythm and blues with like-minded young fanatics. They were the children of refugees who had sailed from the other side of the world to escape their war-torn lands. The beat of the ports of old Europe came straight to Melbourne, where it was nurtured into a sound that was to become uniquely Australian. The musicians who were born here discovered black man's music by listening to radio or exploring their parent's record collection.

Richard was fortunate to work with Keith. Although a good family man now, Keith grew up as a rocker in Wales during the 1950s and early 60s and had seen all the greats live – the Beatles, the Stones, the Animals, Van Morrison and many more. It changed his life forever. When Keith heard Richard was into Chain, he lent the younger man his collection of blues music and Richard was blown away by Howlin' Wolf, Johnnie Lee Hooker, Muddy Waters, Robert Johnson and Leadbelly. This raw gutsy music from the Mississippi delta and Chicago blared out of his Geelong flat. The haunting wails and good-time music of American slavery wove its magic though the rhythm and blues bands of the baby boomers. Together with thousands of his fellow countrymen, Richard underwent the rite of passage of discovering that the black man's blues still speaks to us now. It rails against wage slavery and the empty-headed and crass materialism that surrounds us all. The blues tells us that life's about dancing, loving, fucking, then death, Richard thought as he threw down half a dozen pain killers and fell back into a coma.

Music stirred him that afternoon; he'd left the radio on the ABC. He heard a woman's voice; she was singing a drifty ballad, a beautiful tale of the sea. You could hear the waves in the background. He crawled over the floor and turned up the volume. When the song finished, the DJ announced he was playing highlights of a concert from last weekend called Waves from Warrnambool.

'What's the name of the band!' Richard shouted into the speaker.

The DJ played another song; it was country and western and Richard almost threw up again.

'What's the name of the fucking band!' He grabbed the half-empty whisky bottle at the side of his bed. The DJ spoke of the unique music coming out of the Western District and said if you listened hard you could hear echoes of the Irish and Scottish migrants who settled there over a century ago. He announced it was time to play Julia and the Moonbirds again. Julia's ghostly voice wove out of the speaker.

'It's her! It's her! Julia and the Moonbirds from Portmagee! Julia and the Moonbirds from Portmagee! I've gotta remember her. Julia and the Moonbirds from Portmagee. Where's a fucking pen! Typical, never around when I fucking need one. Julia and the…' Richard crawled around the flat for a pen. 'Ouch! Carpet burns!' He rubbed his bare knees, then collapsed on his back.

The Moonbirds song washed over him. Her voice had the same lament that he'd heard in blues singers; it pierced his young heart. When the song finished, Richard resumed his search but forgot what he was looking for. He found a small bottle of pills and threw down its contents. In his alcoholic stupor, he thought he'd taken more painkillers, but they were sleeping tablets. 'Julia and the…Port…Julia and…Port Campbell…Julia.' The young man fell unconscious.

The next day, teenagers trickled in to Dick's Goods music department to search through the records. Some asked Keith Gould if they had anything by Julia and the Moonbirds.

'Who?' the Welshman asked, 'Julia and the whosits?'

'The Moonbirds,' replied one long-haired, pimply-faced fan.

'Nope. Never fooking heard of them.' When the Welshman saw the disappointed look on the teenager's face, he told him to hang while he checked with the boss. Keith tapped on Richard's office door and walked in. The manager was slumped over his desk, snoring.

'Jeysus, look what the fooking cat dragged in.' Keith laughed to himself then threw a glass of water over Richard.

'Ah, what did you fucking do that for?' Richard shook his head and wiped the water off his pale face.

'You look like death warmed up, you silly boy. I've a question for you.'

'Yeah, what?'

'Have we got anything by Julia and the whosits?'

'The whatsits?'

'No the whosits. Julia and the Moonbirds. We've had a few pubescents coming in this week and asking if we've got anything by them?'

'Nah, never heard of them.' Richard fell back on the desk.

During the rest of the week, more teenagers kept coming in to ask after the band. As their numbers increased, the cash register chimed in Keith's head and he decided to look though the store's record catalogue on file.

'Now, let's see.' Keith pulled a list out of the filing cabinet. 'Julia and the Thingamajigs.' The assistant manager flicked through the paper. 'Julia and the Moonbirds. Julia, Ted Mulrey, nope. The Moondoggys, nope. Ah here's something. "She's My Lady", Johnnie Kelly and the

Moonbirds. the Moonbirds – is that them? I'll give Johnnie a tingle.' Johnnie Kelly was a drinking mate of Keith's.

'Ah, yeah, man, they're a grouse little band of young 'uns from Portmagee. Yep, they backed me up on my latest disc. Yeah, the lead singer's got such elfin features. She's a real spunk. She's got more talent in her little pinky than I have in my whole body. You know, my song's roaring up the Geelong charts thanks to those kids. Meet you down the Grand tonight?'

When Johnnie hung up, Keith's curiosity was aroused even more. He ordered in a couple of hundred of Johnnie and the Moonbirds single, the kids bought them like hotcakes.

Richard Barton's pink nostrils flared when Keith told him about the band. 'The Moonbirds, the Moonbird. Where have I heard that name before? Hmm.' Richard rubbed the red stubble on his chin then drained another whisky for lunch.

That night when he heard Julia's voice on the radio again, Richard bought a six-pack and drove below the huge Western District stars down the highway to Portmagee.

10

Richard's downfall

Crows woke him up at dawn, loud crows; Richard opened his bloodshot eyes to discover his body was stiff and sore after a broken sleep in the back seat of his Valiant. It had rained all night; his car, buffeted by the wind at one stage, threatened to flip over. Now there were these bloody crows! He stuck his dazed head up to the windscreen to watch a battle between the crows and magpies. He'd parked his car below a row of ancient pines on the outskirts of town. It was like watching an old World War II movie of a dogfight between Spitfires and German bombers. This time, the bombers won and the magpies fled the pine trees. Crap team anyway, Richard thought to himself as he rubbed his forehead and slumped out of the car.

The young man was greeted by a gale force wind and an ocean roar like a disturbed bull. A willy-wagtail chatted on top of a nearby paling fence. Richard buttoned up his grey suit top and climbed up to see a huge pond. Black swans fled from their nest when he jumped down and a chorus of frogs added to the pain of his hangover. Kneeling, he groaned as he soaked his head in the pond. Sobered a little, he walked into town to discover everything was closed. A sudden storm forced him to take shelter below the the Star of the West Hotel. Portmagee's streets became rivers. He stared forlornly across the road to see that the Belfast Bakery lights were on, but the shop door was closed. Cat-tail seeds of the Norfolk Island pines rushed and he kicked empty beer cans into the gutter, and watching as the surging water snatched them away.

Marching along, Simon and I were locked in debate over a new song. Our shoulder-length hair flared as we huddled against the ice cruel wind.

'It should go la, la, la, la, la, lulla!' Simon buttoned up his duffel coat.

'No, Mooney, I want it to go la, la, la, la, lulla, la.' I pulled my beanie down over my ears and my lumber jacket collar up around my neck.

As we zoomed up Bank Street, I noticed this lost-looking, tall red-headed stranger outside of the Star of the West. 'Look, Mooney, why don't we leave it up to Julia. After all, she's the one who has to sing it, eh?'

'Because it's our song, Shane. I'm getting sick of her interfering all the bloody time!'

We turned into James Street to be greeted by another blast of the roaring forties. Evans and his mates waited for us on the corner.

Bloody bullies, how do you deal with them? Do you ignore them like your mother says? Do you front them as your father says? Do we walk across the road to avoid them or do we walk up to the arseholes to let them know we're not intimidated? I kept swallowing as my heart pumped fear up into my throat. Simon started to cross the road.

'No, fuck them, Mooney. Let them know they don't scare us!' I waved my friend back to my side.

Evans greeted me with a dollop of spit that stuck to my forehead. Before I knew it, Adams and Whitley had grabbed my arms and Evans started punching me in the stomach. Out the corner of my terrified eye, I saw Simon down on the footpath in a foetal position after that coward Sexton had kicked him in the balls. Evans leered as I squealed like a pig. The burning pain in my stomach shot to the rest of my body. I heard Simon crying but I was powerless.

'What the fuck do you think you're doing?' The red-headed stranger's voice bellowed down the street. His hair blazed like the blades on an Anzac badge, his blue eyes were as wide as the crater on

Tower Hill, his nostrils so big you could drive a horse and buggy up them.

But it didn't intimidate the spawn of Satan, who laughed as he tripped over the wet footpath and fell flat on his face. However, his downfall allowed me to pull free of Adams and Whitley and land a bone-shattering punch in the middle of Evan's ugly mug. The barbarian covered his nose in agony then buckled over after I hit him in the guts.

'C'mon, you scum bag! I've been waiting an eternity for this, you prick!' I hovered over the swine with clenched fists.

The sight of their powerless leader was enough to make the other three run off.

'Let that be a lesson to you!' The stranger raised his head and shook his fist at the fleeing adolescents.

Evans slowly rose with his hands still covering his nose.

'I'll get you for this, McCarthy.' He flinched as I threatened him with another punch.

'Like all cowards, you're no good without your bully boys, are you? Just go and pull yourself, Evans.' I watched him retreat towards Bank Street then went up to check on Simon. The sight of him crying and grimacing set me off. I helped my friend sit up, got down next to him and put my arm around his shoulder. Although I have to admit some of my tears were of triumph – I'd finally got my revenge on the king of arseholes.

The stranger stood next to us like a dog with his tail between his legs.

Eve stormed past suddenly with an enraged look on her stone face. We discovered later on that she'd had another God-almighty row with Julia's father over their daughter.

The rain drove us all back to Freddie King's house, where a sleep-disturbed Julia had just gotten out of bed. She hated the way her parents always argued. Her ruffled red hair gave her the appearance of a windswept lion. She wore one of her father's checkered cotton shirts with crimson stockings. Her long bright-coloured legs reminded

Richard of a flamingo. Her shirt was loosely buttoned so that when she leant forward to us, she revealed the curve of her pale breast. Occasionally, Julia got up to light a cigarette or to throw a log on her father's roaring fire. Sometimes she knelt down in front of the hearth to study the progress of the flames. There were fleeting moments of lucidity like when she settled the dispute over our song by saying she was going to sing it this way!

Richard saw the Moonbirds perform at the Caledonian that night. Despite her otherworldliness, Julia held everyone in the palm of her hand. Her voice soared and screamed through every range of human emotion. She only had to nod to you to put you under her spell. Simon responded with his swirling guitar work. I followed her motioning pelvis to maintain the rhythm of each song. Sue sat in the audience with tears streaming below her black sunglasses. Richard leant back on his chair stunned by her every move. Only Steve ignored her, but drummers always operate in a separate dimension anyhow.

11

The Moonbirds start to fly

We met Richard in the parlour of Seacombe House the next day at noon. A fire chatted away in the hearth as the Moonbirds squeezed together on an ancient couch. The wind in the Norfolk Island pines made the sound of a murmuring tide.

'Barton, Martin and Fargo,' Steve tittered to himself as they sat down.

'You guys need a manager.' Richard sat on a chair directly opposite and put on a face of what he thought was authority, but only succeeded in looking like he was suppressing a fart.

'Oh yeah? Who did you have in mind?' Julia lit up a cigarette and blew her smoke up at the ceiling.

'Um, me actually.' The young man adjusted his thin black tie.

'You must be joking!' Julia laughed. 'From what I've heard of you, you can't even manage your own bowel movement.'

'I've been managing Dick's Goods in Geelong all year.'

'Pah! What, all six months! From what I've heard, Mummy and Daddy set you up and you're a hopeless pisshead who relies on others to do the work for him. Sorry, carrot-top, we're not interested.' Julia rose from the couch.

'Hang on a minute, Julia, let's hear what he has to offer.' Simon remained sitting.

'C'mon, boys, carrot-top's a spoilt dickhead.' Julia made her way to the parlour door.

'Look, just hear me out, OK? I've bought heaps of the single you cut with Johnnie. Thanks to me, it's storming up the Geelong charts.'

'Bull-fucking-shit carrot-top, the kids are making that happen, not you!' Julia threw her cigarette butt into the fire.

'If you've actually studied a carrot, you'll notice the top is green not orange.' Richard grinned as he pointed his long finger towards Julia.

The other Moonbirds laughed.

'Don't point. You'll trip over the fairies!' Steve blurted out.

'Does anyone care for an innocent fellow?' The young man produced a couple of joints from the inside pocket of his suit and smiled like the Cheshire cat.

'Hallelujah! Praise the lord! Miracles do occur!' Steve jumped up to Richard with a big grin.

Our drummer dragged the couch around to face the hearth; before I knew it, we were crowded around the fire smoking. Starlings twittered on the power lines outside.

'The thing is, guys, me and my family have contacts around Melbourne. I reckon if you cut a few more tracks and I hawk them around the big smoke, I'll be able to score a record deal. Ah! The sweet smell of excess.' Richard took a big drag of his joint. 'The thing is that there'll have to be a few changes.'

'Fuck off!' Julia took the joint from Richard's outstretched fingers.

'No, you need to tidy yourself and have a stage presence that appeals to all generations.' Richard's blue eyes glazed over.

'Piss off, red knob! We're not doing a Beatles suit and tie thing. That goody-goody-two-shoes rubbish went out a decade ago. It's the 70s now. All the big bands dress casual, even feral. Look at Led Zepp, Black Sabbath, Deep Purple. Forget it!' Julia leant back on the couch and studied the fire.

'Ah, but you're not like other bands. Your music is unique, so you should have a look that really sticks out.' Richard's eyelids drooped.

'We already have a unique stage presence, Dick. Her name's Julia.'

As I took the joint from Julia's fingers, she smiled at me. The fire crackled on.

'How about changing your name? Don't you think the Moonbirds is too obscure?' Richard lit another joint.

'What did you have in mind?' Simon crouched over towards the fire.

'The Kingsmen. Get it? You're Julia King's men.' Richard handed the joint to Steve.

'Ah, come to Poppa!' Steve took a puff. 'Why don't we call ourselves Foreplay? Better still, why don't we all shave our hair off and call ourselves the Foreskins?'

'The Foreskins!' I cacked myself silly, so did Simon. I tend to get the giggles or verbal diarrhoea when I get stoned. Simon's a classic: he goes silent, then laughs at whatever you say to him. You can state the world's about to end in nuclear war and he'll think it's hilarious.

'The name stays, red knob!' Julia's insistent tone quelled our laughter. 'Have you ever been to Griffith Isle during the equinox? At dusk, the first stars appear, then the sky teems with moonbirds. Thousands upon thousands of the darlings suddenly and silently appear. They've come all the way back from the Aleutian Islands – ten thousand miles. They have no landfall. They journey above or on the water all the way across the Pacific! They return in pairs to the burrow they've made the year before. Moonbirds only have one partner throughout their whole life.'

Julia patted me on the arm, then handed me a joint. 'Matthew Flinders called them petrels because they seemed to walk on water. He said he saw so many of them that they literally blacked out the sky! Imagine that. There you are out in a tiny leaky boat in the middle of Bass Strait and the sky turns black with birds! The word "petrel" goes all the way back to Saint Peter, the fisherman who saw Jesus walking on the water.'

The fire reflected in her fluid brown eyes. 'My grandfather once told me that the moon was created from the earth. The circumference of the Pacific is exactly the same size as the moon. When the moon left, it took with it the only animal that doesn't live on any continent. Granddad said the moonbirds still circle the seas of the moon… Then those bastard whalers and sealers came. The skies were clouded with moonbirds, the shores crowded by seals, the oceans carpeted in whales, but the white dogs came to empty the sky and land, and the only thing heard was the crying wind and abandoned shore. But the moonbirds came back, the children of the moon and the Pacific, they came back to blot out the sun, Saint Peter's birds. Over time, whalers and sealers will be thrown back onto the rubbish tip of history from where they came. For as long as the Earth is blue, the moonbirds will live forever.' She rubbed her eyes, smoked, then handed the joint back to a nodding me.

The fire chatter sounded like a chorus of ancient voices backing Julia up.

'Yep! Yep! Yep! Julia, I get the hint! OK, the name remains the same!' Richard's raised his voice.

'Fuck off, red knob. It's not your decision.' Julia gave him a look to kill.

'OK, OK. Jesus! I sense your negative vibes, Julia. Can I throw my hat into the ring again?' Richard rubbed his large pale forehead.

'Fartin' Barton's mixed metaphor hour!' Steve finished a joint and threw it into the fire.

Simon's red round face split with a toothy white smile.

'While I agree with Shane that Julia has a fantastic stage presence, we can take her and the rest of you even further, so that you really stick out from the pack. All right, forget the suits – even though I think they could be a statement against all the shabbiness that seems to be around us at the moment. You still need to entertain the audience. How about Julia dresses up in even sexier gear and the rest of you wear make-up? Hang on, hear me out, guys !' Richard raised his finger to the ceiling. 'It's true that music is dominated by macho long-haired, hairy-chested strutting studs at the moment. Why not swing the other way?'

'What you mean is dress up like a pack of poofs?' Steve produced a can of beer from his dark mohair coat pocket and started laughing.

'Simon, you've been silent on this matter. What's your opinion?' Richard produced another joint from his coat pocket and handed it to our lead guitarist.

'I'll agree to anything you put in front of me, man!' As he lit the joint up and sucked hard, the rest of the Moonbirds started to titter.

I don't recall much of the rest of that afternoon. All I remember is that the conversation became more abstract and yet somehow, before we all fell asleep on the couch, Richard convinced us that he'd become our manager. I suppose you'll agree to anything when you're stoned.

Sue worked hard on her sewing machine to produce dresses for Julia that showed more cleavage and legs. She helped Simon and me apply our make-up. Steve stuck to his T-shirts, jeans and cowboy boots. We supported Johnnie Kelly in a series of gigs around Geelong and the Western District. We Moonbirds grew our hair longer.

At first, the audience consisted of rockers and cockies who'd come to see Johnnie. Some of them were bemused, even hostile to the Moonbirds. Sometimes Johnnie had to yell at them to shut-up because the Moonbirds were the 'future of rock 'n' roll'.

Our set was half composed of Johnnie's hits and old 50s standards; Julia insisted the other half be made up of Moonbird originals. Rockers and cockies ignored or yelled at us, but others became spellbound by Julia's look and voice. A lot of the rocker and cocky anger was directed Simon and me. With our long hair and make-up, we were quite a sight. Sometimes I couldn't get the mascara off and Dad thought I'd been in another fight. It was so good to know the blackness on my face was now due to pleasure rather than pain.

Then the kids began to trickle in to our concerts, long-haired kids starved of any decent live act, shy at first, because of the burly rockers and cockies. In the beginning, they stood rigid and self-conscious while Julia, Simon, Steve and I threw ourselves into our songs. But the music began to loosen them up and they started to dance and cheer. Meanwhile, we cut more songs on a reel-to-reel tape for Richard to promote. Then, as our manager walked the streets of Melbourne with our music in his briefcase, Johnnie's song made its way up the charts of all the big cities of Australia.

12

The King curse

We were on the road to Melbourne in Freddie's battered old Bedford van. After weeks of tramping through the big smoke, Richard had managed to score us an audition to play a gig at the outer suburban Man from Ironbark Hotel. We motored up the Princes Highway with some optimism because he said the owner of the pub, Ross Trounce, supported local bands that had a unique sound. Ross described our demo tape as half Irish and half heavy rock. It was the first time, with the exception of Julia, that the Moonbirds had ever been to a big city. Julia had gone with Freddie to the Moratorium in May, where a hundred thousand badge-wearing, banner-waving stamping people had taken over the streets of Melbourne.

'I'll never forget it, Shaney. Bourke Street was this huge surging sea of marching protesters of all ages and types. People hung out of the windows of the buildings to smile and give us the peace sign. When the organisers of the march gave the pigs a map of where we intended to march, they put up barricades or blocked our path with mounted pigs. Hundreds of blokes in suits and ties photographed us from the footpath as we marched, but the establishment couldn't intimidate us. When we sat down in the middle of the city streets and listened to Jim Cairns, it was like the Sermon on the Mount. It was so good to hear the complete opposite to the conservative shit we were being fed in the media. The pigs and those bullshit artist journos were so pissed off because there was no violence. It was wonderful knowing that a hundred thousand people felt exactly the same way about the war as me and my Da did. All we were saying is give peace a chance.'

Julia smiled at me as she sang from the front seat of the van, then handed Freddie another beer. They both laughed at his belch that sounded like a truck horn.

Unlike our trip to Geelong, it was a perfect day. Sun filtered through the forest canopies of gum to cast long shadows over the tiny town of Stoneyford. Steve sipped his beer as he pointed to a flock of pelicans sailing across a clear blue sky at Colac. A wedge-tailed eagle circled over our van and gazed down at us outside of Winchelsea.

The first inkling I got of Melbourne was the distant grey sky and huge yellow wall of haze that appeared on the horizon once we were north-east of Geelong. We all stared at a rusted stretch limousine dumped in a paddock outside of Werribee. Then, gigantic dark buildings suddenly loomed over the flat landscape like monsters from another time. The tallest buildings in Portmagee were only two storeys. The outer suburbs stretched forever; everything became so noisy and fast. Every town dweller, dressed in either black or grey, had an anxious look on their face.

The closer we got to the city, the more bewildered Simon and I became, whereas the other three's spirits soared. The only thing Melbourne had in common with Portmagee was that we still experienced four seasons in one day. The rain chased the sun. It was reassuring to know that this giant termite mound of activity hadn't yet conquered the sky.

The Man from Ironbark Hotel sat grandly at the end of the Eastern Freeway at Bulleen. It was one of those double-storey swirling trellis veranda pubs built during the gold rush and, unlike the Stump, it was fully completed a long time ago.

Richard zigzagged up to us as we pulled into the car park. 'Hello, hello, hello, boyshs and girlshs. Lishen, Ross shays youse can play on hish stage for an hour and then he'll letsh youse know, all right?' Our manager took forever to light a cigarette then didn't notice when he set fire to his thumb.

Ross trundled out of the pub door holding a beer carton to his chest. He was a short, skinny, grey-haired, silver-moustached man with skin that stretched like leather over his middle-aged bones. 'Speen a long droive, eh?' Without waiting for a response, the pub owner dropped the carton down on the asphalt then ripped its top off to give us all a long-necked bottle of beer.

Seeing that we'd just travelled close to three hundred miles, we all leapt at the chance for a drink. I don't remember much about our gig that night or what happened the rest of the weekend.

I hazily recall copious amounts of drinking, just managing to play my guitar on stage, running around late at night with no pants on, dancing with a girl with long blonde hair and a low-cut gold dress, lots of laughter and Ross telling me the best decisions made in rock 'n' roll were always made when people are outrageously pissed.

What sticks out about that lost weekend is what happened after I put my arm around Julia's father in the pub to tell him that I loved him. He gave me this huge smile in return and told me nobody had said anything like that to him for a long time. With a pleading look, he made me promise that I'd always be there for his daughter.

'You're the son he never had, Shaney,' Julia chuckled as she put her arms around both of us. 'I'm the daughter you never had, right Dad!'

'Julia…Julia…there's so much I want to tell you…you see…'

'It's all right, Da.' Julia kissed him on his forehead.

'No, it's not all right, my love. You see…I feel so fucking guilty. I'm the father you never had! I've…I've had this illness all my life, love. It comes in spirals.' Freddie half emptied his glass then stared down at the floor. 'I've been to stacks of doctors. None of them can give me an answer. Some say it was the war, some say it was because my father beat the crap out of me when I was young. You see, I sometimes go completely flat, can't sleep for months. It's like some demon comes and steals my soul away. It paralyses me, I stay in my room, lie in bed, keep the curtains drawn, sometimes for months. This helps.' Julia's father bottomed his glass then called for another.

'When I get like that, I'm of no use to anyone. I've been in and out of loony bins for years. I've been zapped by ECT. That's why I've kept my distance from you and your mother, my love. But now that I'm back with you, Jules, I've managed to keep the demons away. I've learnt you've got to keep moving. Sorry, I never wanted to tell you this, Jules.'

'It's all right Da, it's all right.' Julia cuddled her sobbing father to her chest, then gently stroked his hair. 'I understand, Da. You're not alone. I'm the same way. All my life I wondered where it came from. It must be some sort of King curse. Eve's been wanting to send me to a shrink, but I don't want to go. I'm on pills to put me to sleep. I've had these nightmarish nights where I can't drop off until three of four in the morning. The next day I'm rooted, like you, and it goes on for months too. My mind's always chatting away. The only thing that help me is my music, Da, Sue and of course him.' Julia nodded towards me.

'I can see why, love. He's a good kid, isn't he? He hasn't got a mean bone in his body.' A tearful Freddie slowly lifted his head from his daughter's chest then offered me a cigarette.

My love deepened for both of them that night. What was this horrible illness? How could I help? How could I protect them from whatever it was that kept them awake at night? The drunken joyfulness around us didn't matter any more. Two frail souls had revealed their inner demons to me. The death of my mother had taught me that this emotional honesty was true existence and that everything else was superficial. I made a pledge to help them in whatever way that I could and try to overcome my teenage awkwardness to be their chest to lean on. But there were still a few hurdles I had to leap.

13

The desert moon

Thunder-blue clouds marched across Bass Strait towards us. Freddie gulped down his beer and Simon mumbled something about him slowing down. As usual, Freddie and Julia never listened to any word of caution. Wind gusts blew debris across the highway. Lightning zapped the empty paddocks around us. Julia started to laugh. A pulsating sun disappeared behind shadows of rain and the old Bedford van creaked as it was buffeted by the southern winds. The dark bulging sky rumbled.

Freddie turned the heater up and rubbed the windscreen with his chamois. Gum trees swayed and bowed beside the road. Steve snored on the floor – an atomic bomb could have gone off and he'd still be in the land of nod.

The sky in front of us turned silver. When the road vanished in a downpour of rain, Freddie finally slowed down. He chuckled when Simon said he should pull over and wait for the storm to blow itself out.

Freddie leant into the windscreen to make out the white lines in the middle of the road. I don't know how he did it because we were completely surrounded by a thick cloud of fog. I couldn't see a damn thing, yet still he edged us on. Julia handed her father another can.

I gave out a yelp when I saw some heads with horns suddenly lunge at my window. Julia wet herself when we realised we'd driven into a herd of cattle. A farmer raised his walking stick and shouted something to us. Whatever it was, Freddie ignored him and kept pushing on. Simon gave me a pleading look. I was just about to say something when the mist in front of us lightened. Thank God. Hopefully we'd made it through. But it turned out to be the lights of an oncoming car. The last thing I recalled was the unholy sound of metal and glass smashing, then Freddie's ungodly sigh.

The ocean hissed away, rain dripped from a hole in the roof onto my face. Simon knelt over me, pleading and I could hear Steve cursing as he tried to kick his way out of the back door of the van. Simon's cry blended with the tide to sound like a far away song that beckoned me from the cold nothingness that was overtaking my body.

I'd reached a tranquil state of indifference where Julia and Freddie were showing me the way. I tried to keep up with them. Julia's long red locks merged with the waves to motion like seaweed, her pale features sank below the foaming water to become coral. Freddie's summoning white hand slipped below the surface; he smiled at us before he sank into the kelp forest on the sea floor. Seaweed wrapped around my ankles. The song from the shore made me hesitate and I tapped Julia on the shoulder, then heard this dull, clanking sound – Steve had finally booted the van doors open.

Julia's hospital face reverted to the look of her ancestors: her Aboriginal great-grandmother dumped on the beach by the whalers, her Scottish great-grandmother orphaned after the shipwreck, her mother's look when she lost her husband. After Julia came out of her concussion, she cried for days, then when there were no tears left her features set rock hard. It turned out that Freddie had had a head-on with an off-duty drunk copper who was on the wrong side of the road. The farmer knew the copper always drove like a madman on this stretch of the highway after the six o'clock swill and had tried to warn us.

Freddie was gone. Mad, good-time Freddie, just at the time where he'd managed to reconnect with his daughter. I was devastated. I was going to miss the bugger; he was the only adult who truly encouraged the Moonbirds to pursue the dream. Others were scornful or indifferent, whereas Freddie was always there for the band. I felt as close to him as I did to my own dad.

But Julia was the one I feared for. Her father's death sent her off the deep end and how was I going to help to bring her back? Sue was there for her everyday, thank God; gentle-talking, always-listening, hand-holding, wonderful, loving Sue.

Sometimes we caught the same bus along the coast road to Warrnambool hospital. The trouble was, Richard and Eve visited Julia every day as well. Richard kept mumbling a series of almost indecipherable clichés, whereas Eve sat at the foot of the bed in stony silence. I wanted to cut through Richard's verbal diarrhoea and Eve's oppressive silent melancholia to share with Julia my ways of coping with the death of a parent. But Julia didn't respond to my overtures anyway. I so wanted to tell Richard to shut the fuck up and for Eve to actually say something, anything, but I was still an awkward teenager.

The only positive to Freddie's death at that time was that during that long-gone winter I got closer to Sue. As the sea swelled like burnt milk and the earth turned her southern axis away from the sun, we had many a heart to heart along the coast road. I learnt what a selfless person she was. Instead of using her winnings in an art competition to buy much-needed painting equipment, Sue, to please Julia, bought a guitar and joined the Moonbirds. She told me she was terrified every time she got up on stage, and that she was so happy that Simon and I had joined the band. Sue stressed that Julia needed the company of fellow creative souls who understood her, not cretinous greed merchants like Richard.

Freddie's funeral took place in the old bluestone church of St John's in Regent Street on the outskirts of town. The priest went on with the usual tripe. It always strikes me that the person who conducts the final ceremony usually never knows the deceased, and that you can be on this planet for a long time but a complete stranger sums up your life's journey in twenty to thirty minutes, if you're lucky. Thank god Johnnie Kelly was asked to come up and say a few words.

Johnnie said his first memory of Freddie was of him flying down the main streets of Geelong at night in a shopping trolley. Johnnie and Freddie used to have shopping trolley races after a marathon session at the Scottish Chief's Hotel. Patrons of the pub used to punt on who'd win and pretty soon it became known as the Geelong Grand Prix. These midnight races came to an abrupt end when a police car chased a whooping, flying Freddie all the way down to the Barwon River. When the police dragged him out of the water for being drunk and disorderly, Freddie argued that there was nothing disorderly about it; the grand prix was a well planned public event. Years later, the story transmogrified around the streets of Geelong that Freddie was nabbed for speeding because the trolley was over the speed limit. Apparently to this day, whenever the river level drops down, you can still see it rusting away.

Johnnie told us how Freddie celebrated his twenty-first birthday with Italian prisoners of war, drunk as a skunk in the sands of North Africa. After his ship ran the gauntlet of the Luftwaffe and dropped its supplies off at Bardia, Freddie scoured the streets desperate for a drink. He was just about to give up when he came across some Australian troops escorting Italian prisoners off to a camp. He noticed one of the Italians had a tank on his back with a small hose on its side. Freddie first thought that it was one of those newfangled flame-throwers people were talking about. 'Vino,' was the response when he gestured to ask the Italian what he had on his back.

He said it was one of the best nights of his life. He and the Aussies couldn't speak a word of Italian, they knew no English, but somehow they discovered it was Freddie's twenty-first. They ended up finding a comfortable sand dune on the outskirts of town then got stuck into the vino. Then came the African moon. Freddie didn't know what it was when it started to rise over the desert. Was it a distant battle? Searchlights? The lights of Cairo? The brow of a god? No, it was a giant desert moon and, coming from England where the night sky's obscured by mist or smoke, he'd never seen anything like it before.

Julia's father said it was a life-altering night; under the dazzling moonlight, he discovered the enemy were just like us. The Italians made it clear that they thought Hitler and Mussolini were buffoons and that they were dying to get back home to their wives and make more bambinos. He also couldn't get over the Australians: they were so approachable, irreverent and informal, the complete opposite to his countrymen. Plus they had their priorities right, they loved a drink, a yarn and a good laugh.

Every subsequent Australian he met during the war was exactly the same; it made him want to migrate. The big Australian moon always reminded him of that glorious African night with all of its joyful connotations of youth, freedom and joy. Those last three words were always what Freddie tried to aspire to, so Johnnie said he wouldn't want anyone to grieve for him for too long. His mate finished by saying Freddie was Liverpool Irish and everyone was invited back to the Caledonian for a wake. The packed crowd of St John's all had smiles on their faces, except for Julia and Eve.

Poor Julia wailed like a banshee when they lowered her father's coffin into the ground at Portmagee's graveyard. I kept swallowing my heart as it threatened to burst out of my chest. Everything was grey that day, the lousy rain-swept sky, the sea, the angels, the Celtic crosses, our souls. Freddie wouldn't want this, I told myself, and remembered that pledge I gave to him seemingly light years ago at the Man from Ironbark Hotel. I decided to go up to Julia; it was surprisingly easy to brush by a protesting Richard because he was comatose anyway.

Julia knelt in the mud, staring at her father's grave; Sue was down on her knees next to her. I stood behind them and placed both my hands on their shoulders. Simon and Steve held their umbrellas over us. I didn't say a thing. What could you say? Sue looked up to me and gave me a faint smile. Julia didn't respond at all. I only half listened to the priest's words and looked over to my mother's grave. I wondered where she was now and if she'd met Freddie yet. Her death had shattered any scrap of belief I might have had in the church.

Mary gave me an illustrated children's Bible when I was a little tacker; back in ancient Israel, God appeared to be everywhere. He seemed to have lost his way last century – fallen in the mud of the

Western Front, choked in the gas at Auschwitz, vapourised in the boiling tar of Hiroshima, hidden in the jungles of Vietnam. Unable to stop kids from getting the hell beaten out of us, not there to take care of our parents. To paraphrase Thomas Hardy, Christianity's had two thousand years; it's time to give something else a go. I know Freddie would agree with me. I can see his nodding, beaming face crinkled by cigarette smoke, his eyes drunk on the joy of love.

14

Pea Soup blues

She chose a remote group of rocks out at Pea Soup beach, late at night, figuring everyone would be at her dad's wake. She took her mother's carving knife from the top drawer in the kitchen and walked out of her silent home. She figured she'd do it after smoking a pack of cigarettes. She chain-smoked and stared at the dark wild waters of Bass Strait. She'd entered that realm that a handful of us enter, a place where everyday thoughts disappear, a state of hopelessness, a place where death hovered close by like a long lost friend. Where you seek to embrace it. As Julia chanted, 'Death, death, death', the waves echoed her call, even encouraged it. She drew heavily on her last cigarette and then began to carve away on her wrist.

I was too pissed to go home. I needed a walk and some fresh air. A few dry retches warned me I was in danger of vomiting and when I vomit, I go all night both ends. I'd recently slept in my own chunder; woken up with it caked in my hair and face, with a savage headache that took days to go. The humiliation of it too. Dad had made it a point to show Mike the next morning. There I was in all my naked, crutch-gripping, Technicolor glory. Never again.

I'd managed to extract myself from Richard's embrace, Johnnie's stories, my father's endless dirges, Steve, playing his drumsticks on the bar of the Caledonian. The smoke inside the pub was as thick as a London fog. The fresh air hit me like a truck when I finally stumbled outside then staggered down Sackville Street. I leant on a lamp post and looked up at the forest of silver stars. A crescent moon paddled towards Portland.

Skin can be tough. It had taken Julia a long time to cut through to her vein. In frustration, she'd tried to drive the knife into her broken heart. She'd held it as far away from her chest as possible then attempted to plunge it in but the knife didn't pierce her skin. When she went back to her wrist, her blood started to trickle onto the rocks. She sighed, then smiled at her progress. Come now, death. Come now, my old companion. Tears blurred her vision. A series of images came to her exhausted brain; one that stuck was when she was a skinny twelve-year-old in her bikini on her surfboard. She'd love to swim at East Beach and stare into the crowd of holidaymakers in the hope that her father was watching her. He never showed up; it didn't matter, for she'd soon be joining him.

Pea Soup sounds insane tonight; the waves are smashing onto the rocks. I puffed and heaved as I staggered up the hill towards it. Venus blazed like a lantern over Deen Maar, the island floating like a giant plank in the moonlight. Lightning flickered on the horizon. Bass Strait was in an uproar; waves born in Antarctica were furious at encountering their first landfall. The bombardment had woken the sleeping moonbirds into a disturbed chatter. It was the first time I'd heard them this late at night. Then I saw her hunched silhouette.

'Julia!' I heard this hiss like a cornered snake as she swung her body up towards me.

'Fuck off!' Julia snarled then pointed the knife at me.

I made my way slowly towards her. 'Julia! Julia! It's me, Shane!' My teeth chattered as the wind threatened to knock us over.

'Shane! Shane! Shane! Fuck off!' Julia's withering stare in the moonlight almost made me stop for a minute, but I had a belly full of beer to cloud my judgement so I stepped up to her. 'Go the fuck away, Shane.' Julia cut the air with her knife.

'Julia! Please let me help you, sweetie. C'mon, it's freezing out here!' My open palm throbbed after Julia stabbed it. 'Fuck! Whatya do that for!' I felt the first drop of rain on my face. 'C'mon, Julia, let me take you home. Christ, you're bleeding. Let me bandage it. I'll get a fire going.'

Waves sprayed around us.

'Leave me alone, Shane! Please! I've had enough! Can't you see that! I've lost the closest person to me on this planet!' Her pleading look was the same look Freddie gave me that night in the pub in Melbourne.

'So have I, Julia. Believe me, I know how you feel.' It started to pour. 'Besides, Freddie made me promise to look after you. He wouldn't want this. He'd want you to move on. C'mon, Jules, it's pissing down.' I wiped the rain off my face. 'Julia, you're our dream. We'd be nothing without you. Think of the band, think of the way Freddie threw his support behind us, think of Sue… she'd be devastated without you. So would I. C'mon, we've got to get out of this bloody rain.'

I cleaned her wrist, then used Mary's bandages; Julia insisted that she wasn't going to a doctor. When I gave her my pyjama top and tucked her into my bed, she asked for a hug. I patted her long hair and kissed her forehead. Her body shook as she sobbed. She clutched me as I hugged her. Our bodies swayed together.

Pea Soup roared in the distance like a wild beast denied one of its victims. I thought of how desperately lonely Julia must have been out there. Through her sobs, I whispered to her how I tried to cope with the death of my mother. You don't recover; you never recover from the death of someone close to you. There's always an aching hole in your life. Mum and I used to have heart to hearts; I don't have them with anyone any more with maybe the exception of Sue. It's painfully cruel how a living, breathing loved one can be suddenly snatched from you.

I told Julia how that at the actual time of Mary's death I felt a part of her spirit enter mine. 'Mary lives on in here.' I patted my heart. 'She lives on in my blood and through her love. It's the same with Freddie, Julia – you're a part of him, he's a part of you. He's probably being nagged by Mary in the hereafter for drinking too much, but is there alcohol in the hereafter? Probably not. How boring.'

I shut up, thinking I'd blabbed too much. Julia had stopped crying. Her long hair was fragrant with rain, life-saving rain from the Southern Ocean that had made Julia drop her knife and forced us both indoors.

I heard Mike talking in his sleep in the bedroom next door. Dad came home in the early hours of the morning to accidentally kick the cats then play Robert Johnson on our stereo, his ghostly voice wailing through the gale force wind. Julia's breathing slowed to the sound of the tide on a summer's night. Pea Soup still bellowed and bands of rain battered our roof, but I didn't care. I had the woman who I adored at rest in my arms and the bitter sweet music of life nearby.

15

By the fire

Our part of the planet turned its back on the sun; swollen Bass Strait blanketed Portmagee in grey. Old street signs flapped, rust ate our boats and cars, trees threatened to fall into the boggy soil. The north desert wind battled the roaring forties. Locals admitted the wind's struggle made them restless; the lack of sun turned them melancholy.

Julia passed the winter beside Sue's fireplace in Grant Street. They talked as two fellow spirits do. Both had what Shakespeare called the 'seething brains' of creativity. Sue and Julia soared up into boundless realms of the imagination. Their conversation, not distracted by the everyday, explored their deep reverence for ideas and possibilities; affirmed by each other's love, I was privileged to be part of it. Julia's attempt at suicide was raised without judgement, so was her deep sorrow over her father. What else could Sue and I do but offer our unconditional love?

Solstice day arrived, Julia's eighteenth birthday, and Sue and I managed to pry her out of Grant Street and into the Caledonian, where Bernie, the silver-bearded publican, had built a huge fire and decorated the counters and tables with wattle flowers. The bright yellow flowers always remind me of little suns that blaze defiantly against the grey despair of winter.

The interior of the pub, with its fire, flowers and the publican's beaming face, was a heavenly distraction from the recent intensity. A feline Julia sat silently next to the hearth. Sue went up to her, gave her a hug and wished her a happy birthday. The rest of the Moonbirds crowded around a nearby table; Steve plied us all with drinks while Richard held up the bar with Russell Ives and his drunken mates, and even our original guitarist, Alex Fitzsimmons, joined us. Julia half smiled at Sue's present. It was a framed picture she'd taken of the Moonbirds going full throttle in Warrnambool. The gleam came back to Julia's eyes after she unwrapped my present; it was the Beatles' *White Album.*

How do you recover from depression? Do you fully come back? All I know was when I saw the shine in her eye. She'd waded back from that nightmarish shore out at Pea Soup beach. She told me later on that the knot in her stomach loosened that night. The invisible monster of grief took a holiday.

Freddie once told his daughter that Churchill too had suffered from the Black Dog. The man who'd stood up to the devil incarnate, Hitler, had once said that, 'If you find yourself moving through hell, keep moving.' Good advice for a parent to give their child. Mind you, Julia also said the grog helped that night as well.

My dad's band played all night and Bernie relaxed the rules about women drinking separately in the ladies' lounge so that Eve and the other mothers of our tribe could join us. Bernie's suspension of the archaic custom of women and men drinking separately was the first of many rules I was to observe broken for the better as a teenager. The Victorian era was in its death throes.

Dad's band did 'Tam Lin', that ancient and curious song from the dawn of time about an angry fairy queen who abducts the main protagonist lover and turns him into a dream. With its swirling Celtic rhythm and the belief that the supernatural world exists beside us, it's a song that's always haunted me. You don't need to pray at an altar or partake in a ceremony to commune with the other world; all you need to do is walk through the night.

Simon slung his guitar on; Steve pulled out his drumsticks and drummed the table as Captain Starlight's fiddle player, Terry Farley, jumped up onto the counter to weave a shivering backbone solo. The band's banjo player Max Hayes's smile was as wide as Bass Strait while Dad chanted away with his eyes shut. I lifted a spare guitar from the stage and Captain Starlight jammed with the Moonbirds to extend 'Tam Lin' forever. The Caledonian crowd sang, danced and clapped. The only two who kept themselves removed were Julia and her mother, Eve, but even their rock-like faces glowed after a while.

We invited the spirits of the otherworld to our tiny town of light trailing on the black waters of the southern ocean. Scattered bones stirred along our shipwreck coast and the wind cried over the Portmagee graveyard. I stared out of the window across Bank Street to see Freddie smiling down proudly at us in the form of a vaporous full moon.

16

Melbourne blues

As an eastern spine bill darts around the grevillea bush in my driveway below a clear suburban sky, I'm taken back to the spring of forty years ago, where the wild flowers bobbed next to a swollen Moyne river. My pudgy middle-aged body transforms into the skinny frame of a teenager as I pluck a bunch of vibrant blue and gold native flowers and give them to Julia before we depart on a journey that will lead us to the other side of the world. She gives me a quick kiss then orders me to get into the gold Land Rover Richard's parents bought him for his nineteenth birthday. Our eyes squint as Richard's car hums along the endless flat roads of the Western District where we developed a reputation from our last tour. Marketing us as the band that backed up Johnny Kelly on his huge hit 'She's My Lady', Richard got us gigs in Hamilton, Horsham, as far north as Mildura, as far west as Robe.

Simon and I wrote songs in the back seat of the Land Rover. Aside from Julia, there were plenty of things to inspire us. We camped beside the Grampians, below a burning canopy of stars, to hear the chatter of the first inhabitants; when we saw Min Min lights near Bordertown, Julia explained they were spirit lights.

At Robe, I heard my dead grandfather play his harmonica on Long Beach at dusk; it was his favourite fishing spot. We wrote about the blue lake of Mt Gambier, the giant red gums of the Murray, the ancient rainforests of the Otways and driving up into the never-ending blue dome of a sky after a storm.

My love of Julia and the country seeped through every song. She still collaborated with us when there was a need to bring our stuff back down to earth.

For example, Simon was strumming a new song singing, 'In the meadow I'm a dreaming.'

Julia shot back, 'Before they threw me in the loony bin.'

It pissed us off, but after a while we reluctantly acknowledged her suggestions always worked.

Some look back on the 60s and 70s as an easy time for youth, but they forget just how bloody hard the bands worked. The Moonbirds performed hundreds of times in all kinds of venues in the Western District, then the rest of Victoria, from the dingy and dusty local hippy hall of St Andrews to the TF Much Ballroom in Fitzroy. We'd play non-stop for hours, taking Richard's uppers to keep us going. Sometimes it was sheer torture.

First of all, you had to win a pissed crowd over, then hold their attention. Thank God for Julia. She held the audience in the palm of her hand with her powerful voice, gymnastic dancing and skimpy dresses. Simon and I grew a bit more fearless behind our masks of make-up, then there was always good old Steve, pounding away and ready to jump on any dropkick who gave us a hard time. Crowds seethed in the darkness around us, but we sweating four became one under the stage lights' glare. When our audiences started to clap, cheer and scream, Julia smiled and her beaming features inspired us to dig even deeper. We lost many a good night's sleep but hung onto our dream.

Sue stayed in Portmagee painting away to the song of the waves which reminded her she wasn't part of the everyday. She was prone to headaches now and then; her parents put her symptoms down to her intense creativity. The dissolute Richard replaced Sue's steadying influence over Julia with more alcohol and drugs. Steve noticed my concern one night after a gig when I watched Julia and Richard take off in a taxi rather than continue their usual partying with the Moonbirds.

'Don't worry, Macca. One thing I've noticed about life is that beautiful, smart women always end up with an arsehole.' Steve rubbed his thick mop of black hair with a towel then handballed me a stubby of beer. 'Now, when you and Simon take off your poofy make-up, we'll go out and get snakes hissed.'

I felt betrayed when I saw the back of Julia's red forest of hair disappear into the dark streets of Melbourne. But thankfully I was in good company. We went on a pub crawl through Richmond and ended up in the Corner Hotel, where we were stunned by a mean blues band called Carson. The lead singer's raspy voice and hypnotic harmonica, together with the band's swamp, took my beer-sodden body off to a dancing state of joy. Steve kept feeding me stubbies and told me he'd felt like he was in a dream. Simon stared at the band with a smile the size of the Sea of Tranquillity on his big moon face. I ended up having a drunken conversation with a gnome-like man, Mike Wositzki, who claimed he'd just started up his own record company called Toadstool and was on the lookout for new Aussie acts. He gave me his card and I slipped it into my shirt pocket.

We zigzagged back to our motel that night with me in the middle being propped up by my two good mates, gasbagging about women. Seeing that Simon and I were still virgins, I doubt the veracity of our statements. We smoked, drank (somehow Steve kept performing his magic trick of producing beer from beneath his duffel coat), and we mumbled until a huge Melbourne sun came out to flood the city with red and gold flares.

I felt better at our next gig in the knowledge that I had the sympathetic ear of both Simon and Steve. The Moonbirds kept making inroads into the Melbourne music scene. We rented a two-bedroom flat in Brunswick from my uncle Brian. Julia and Richard shared one bedroom, the rest of the Moonbirds the other. It was always quiet and dark in the other bedroom. A silent, pale Julia sometimes joined us to watch the telly; she only ever came alive those days when she was on a stage.

17

Up in the stratosphere

Richard hawked our tape around the streets of Melbourne. But the men in suits showed little interest. So much for the great myth that businessmen are great risk-takers. Our manager underwent the humiliating experience of sitting in front of po-faced, hair-rinsed nonentities who usually suffered one only song, two if Richard was lucky, and then they icily showed him the door. EMY told him rock 'n' roll was dead now that the Beatles had broken up. Europa records told him kids weren't interested in Australian music, and besides the local market was too small to sustain a local act.

'Have you heard of Daddy Cool, Spectrum, the Master's Apprentices, Billy Thorpe, the Zoot, the Twilights, you todger?' Richard shouted to a suit as he was ushered out through yet another door.

Virgo records said that guitar music was on its last legs. Megaphone records told Richard whoever heard of a rock band with a female lead singer?

Richard came back to Uncle Brian's flat to scratch yet another company off his list. One thing I'll give him, until then, he never lost spirit and always had faith in us, or more likely in Julia. He came to the bottom of his record company list one day smoking a joint, when Steve suddenly looked up from our only piece of furniture, a mattress on the floor.

'Macca…what was the name of the gnome you spoke to the other night at the Corner?'

What gnome? I thought to myself.

Richard steered his dilated blue eyes towards me. I'd forgotten all about the gnome. Then I remember he'd put his calling card in my shirt pocket. Which one did I wear that night? I vaguely recalled I was wearing my blue Miller shirt. But where the bloody hell had I put it? I looked at a mountain of clean laundry that Richard had hauled back from the laundromat. He was our chief cook and bottle-washer after Julia made it painfully obvious to us boys of the 60s that she wasn't prepared to be our domestic slave. The mountain toppled as I discovered my shirt at the bottom. The gnome's business card turned out to be a mashed lump in my pocket. 'Shit! Shit! Shit!' I shouted as I threw the shirt back on the floor.

'Good on you, Macca! So that's what it was that shredded all over our clothes. Our bloody future!' Steve went to our bar fridge in the kitchen, pulled out a beer and laughed.

'Shane, Shane, now listen to me very carefully. Can you remember the gnome's name?' Richard puffed frantically away on his joint.

'Frodo!' Steve chuckled out in the kitchen.

'That's a hobbit, you drongo!' Simon got up from the mattress to tidy up the mess of clothes.

'Grumpy. Hey, remember the old joke? Snow White got into the bath feeling grumpy, so Grumpy got out.' Our drummer chortled in the kitchen.

I tried to turn my mind back to that hazy night at the Corner Hotel.

'Fungi, fungi, it had something to do with fungi.'

'Well, that narrows things down a bit.' Steve dropped a thunderous belch.

'Toadstool. It's Toadstool! I'll ring up directory assistance.' Richard flicked through the Telecom white pages. 'Hello, hello, can you give me the number for Toadstool. Thanks. Hello, is that Gnome? Shit, sorry, is that the manager? I believe you've been talking to one of my clients.'

Before we knew it, we were nervously auditioning for a record contract with Mike Wotzitski. He and Richard shared several joints together as they watched us.

With his vest, long shaggy hair, and small features, he was the spitting image of a character straight out of *Lord of the Rings*. His head bobbed like the toy dogs you see on the back of car dashboards as he listened to our entire set. 'Yeah, it's cool, man. I've just come back from swinging London. You cats are right out there, man. You see, there's a big blues and folk scene going on over there, with really cosmic bands like Cream and Fairport Convention. Ever heard of them?' Mike blew smoke out of his nostrils.

We shook our heads.

'That's unreal, man! Probably because you're a bush band you're still in contact with your roots. Rock's getting back to its roots. You guys have managed to tap into the future of music. It's Celtic and black.'

'So what do you think, man?' As Richard spoke, I'd noticed his features had gone feral since he'd become our manager. With his long red hair and beard, he looked like a Viking.

'Well, you're so avant-garde, man. You're so way out, you're in. Let's cut a few discs together.'

After much partying, we decided to release 'Great Ocean Road' as our first single. Mike gave the job of producer to Tim Keays, lead singer of legendary Australian band the Yellow Mondays (they got their name from a species of cicada) who'd had hit after hit in Oz, but imploded after four gruelling tours of America. The Yellow Mondays had cut their last record in the Abbey Road studio and used to see The Beatles walk by sometimes. Tim reckoned George Harrison dressed and looked like an American Indian.

Our producer was a wealth of knowledge; his first bit of advice was never go to overseas unless you've got a hit, and if the band has any personality problems, make sure you sort them out before you head off, otherwise it's a sure fire recipe for a disaster. I remember Julia played a mean harmonica on our first single. We got an invite onto Hitscene on Channel Two (a government-owned station that was prepared to back new, local music) and mimed our way through our first hit. It made it up all the way to number eighteen. Tim got us back into the studio to ask us if we had anything more raunchy. Simon and I shook our heads but Julia picked up a guitar from the floor and belted out her song 'The Teacher'. It was full of love towards her father. Tim's eyes lit up and his nostrils flared; he could smell our first number one.

We all got incredibly pissed. Our tiny flat in Brunswick burst with people, to the stage where complaining neighbours joined in. Mike, Tim and Richard shared a Zeppelin-sized joint to soar rapidly up into the stratosphere. People from Toadstool records, our fans, reporters, people we'd never met before, all chatted, drank and laughed; the grog flowed and the faces glowed. Julia was nowhere to be seen; I tapped on her bedroom door then stepped in to see her studying the spring rain lashing against her window.

'How are you, Jules?' I closed the door to the broiling mass of humanity then hovered in her doorway.

'OK, Shaney!' she whispered back to me and revealed that she was scared of the momentum we'd created and had a bad feeling about where it would all end up.

I sat down on the bed next to her and told her she thought too much, that Shakespeare once wrote somewhere that 'there is nothing good or bad, only thinking makes it so', and that she should be happy now she'd reached her dream. How many people managed to achieve that in their lifetime?

Julia gave me that devastating smile that was so rare lately, and stroked my hair. We drank from a bottle of red wine she kept by the side of her bed and talked; about our dead parents, our music, our fears, what an arsehole Richard Barton was, and how she should keep him at arm's length. Julia produced another bottle and refilled our glasses; after we toasted the success of the Moonbirds, she placed her pointer finger on my lips and told me to shut my mouth.

It was almost dawn when people left the party. A gentle September light trickled into Julia's bedroom. She took her eyes off the window and stared at me. She slipped her top off, lay back on the bed, then held her open hand up to me. I took my shirt off and leant across the bed to stroke and kiss the angry scar on her wrist. Julia tugged me towards her. We embraced, I rocked her in my arms; she unzipped my pants, peeled hers off and guided me into her. I'll never forget her beautiful sighs, her cries that I was so gentle. I kissed her half-shut eyelids, and swayed my pelvis to her rhythm. She showed me how to get on top of her and go deep inside. After more kissing, she straddled me. I saw her flat tummy ride my pleasure, felt her long red hair tickle my face like a gentle breeze, her small firm breasts brush against my chest. Towards the end, I watched the woman I worshipped nakedly circle my love. Julia's whole body eventually shuddered; she gave out a deep sigh, collapsed next to me, then slowly fell asleep in my clutching arms. My limbs turned numb. I couldn't sleep, but I didn't care. Her breath reminded me of the sound of the summer tide at night on East Beach. I'd only been in the city for a few months but I missed my home town already.

The Brunswick rain eased into drizzle as my tired mind composed new songs to Julia. Those in-between moments – dawn, dusk, after an emotional event, or recovering from a hangover – are the best times to write. I felt that I'd shed my skin and transformed into another person. We sipped more wine and enjoyed each other for the rest of the day while Simon and Steve snored in the bedroom next door. Richard raged on at another party somewhere in the snowy Dandenongs. I stayed her hand when she wanted to sniff some of his cocaine.

The old Julia returned when she gave an energetic performance and giggly interview on *Countdown* the following night. Julia and the Moonbirds were presented with their first gold record while a barely standing Richard smoked behind the cameras with the green-eyed monster stare of jealousy, his drug-fuelled brain silently mocking our happiness.

18

Aztecs and Mexicans

They were the best years of my life. Julia and I were lovers and the Moonbirds conquered Australia with a string of number one hits. I never thought it would be possible to be so close to another human being. After I moved into her bedroom, Richard rented a flat nearby and tried to entice our lead singer out with all kinds of chemical substances; but she didn't respond. Julia wasn't one to play games with your emotions; she always made her intentions obvious. We made love every night, even after a big gig or a long ride in Richard's Land Rover.

I wrote heaps of songs about her and the exquisite way she gave herself to me. Not only did we share each other's body and mind, but Julia took a stronger role in our songwriting. In our spare moments, Simon and I would get out our acoustic guitars, eyeball each other, then write; now Julia would sit next to me and join in. I could tell Simon was annoyed, but hey, I was never going to object to the woman I adored enriching our songs with her maverick ideas. Plus it's an inevitable rite of passage – when you find your first lover, you sometimes overlook your best friend.

Richard drove us up the Hume Highway to Sydney, where we played in the Coogee Bay Hotel. It was the first time any of us had ever seen the Pacific. The blue water and Mediterranean climate was such a contrast to the grey ocean and wild weather of our home town. The people were different too; their Aussie accents were stronger and very nasal. They were louder and more hedonistic than we Mexicans, the nickname they gave to Victorians because we came from south of the border.

We didn't mind the hedonism; I remember the Moonbirds spent a lost weekend doing a pub crawl of the Rocks. Julia and I ended up yarning with some World War I veterans at the Fortunes of War Hotel; we promised to remember them and wrote a song about the beautiful old fellas and incorporated it into our set. That song about diggers sometimes upset the hippies in our audience, but stuff them, we thought, every Australian had a family member who fought in a war. I recall the Moonbirds could barely stand or talk when we ended up below the Harbour Bridge for the first time in the drizzle.

Many things stick out in our tours around Australia: the rolling green hills of Adelaide, Stephen claiming he saw the Nullarbor nymph near Eucla (a naked spirit that wails as she runs around the desert at night), a huge fat full moon that turned night into day in the middle of the desolate Nullarbor, the unique blue of the tropical Brisbane sky, the snow falling on Mt Wellington in Hobart during summer and the Aurora Australis in Deloraine, Tasmania. Julia described the lights in the night sky as being like a giant monarch butterfly. The songs flowed from our excited young hearts and minds.

Our enthusiasm was part of a national celebration in December 1972: Australia elected its first Labor government in twenty-three years; the grey men finally lost power and with them the greyness that was the Australia of our childhood. Gough Whitlam brought our troops home from Vietnam. John Lennon sang, 'War is over if you want it.' Our country underwent a cultural renaissance.

We started to produce quality movies for the first time in many years, people spoke of the unique Australian light on the screen. Daggy, sometimes semi-pornographic local soap operas blossomed on the telly. Australian writers started to sell in the thousands, Australian audiences began to love our painters who, from World War II onwards, produced mythical images that could only come from this country but were nevertheless universal. Our bands made music that was just as good as what came from overseas, if not better than.

The Australian voice became widespread in the media for the

first time. It was embarrassing before the 70s, because there were few Australian movies around and, if there were, the lead actors were imports from Britain and America. When they attempted our Australian accent, the English sounded cockney, the Yanks, Irish. Even our newsreaders had Pommy accents. In the picture theatres, people stood up and sang 'God Save the Queen' along with the Royal Grenadiers on the big screen before they saw a movie! (God save Johnnie Rotten.) We liked to think that Australia was cutting the apron strings with the 'mother country'.

And then there was Sunbury, where a plethora of local acts entertained thousands of mind-altered kids. There's a theory going around that this was where the unique Australian rock 'n' roll sound was born. That meaty, electronic blues, which you hear in Midnight Oil, Hunters and Collectors, ACDC, Powderfinger, Jet, and so on, all goes back to the bands that performed at Sunbury, the recently departed Billy Thorpe in particular. Again, Billy was another English migrant kid who pioneered the rhythm and blues sound.

While the Woodstock kids sang about peace and love, our kids chanted SMP! Suck, more, piss! I should know – I was there with them, so were Steve, Richard and Simon, all of us, squillions of us, (Julia was in our tent; she didn't think much of Billy Thorpe and the Aztecs), sunburnt, dehydrated, pissed as newts, screaming out for more. The Moonbirds were fortunate enough to play at the last Sunbury. We saw the big punch-up between ACDC and Deep Purple; it was like something out of a Wild West movie.

Bon Scott was so transfixed by Julia that he modelled his haircut and stage act on her. She told him to piss off several times when he tried to grope her. I nearly got into a stoush with him; he was as flash as a rat with a gold tooth. The man's copious drinking made us all look like teetotalers.

When a young Johnny Rotten saw ACDC play live in England, he was hit for a six and began imitating Bon's style and the way he performed on stage.

Another influence the Moonbirds had was make-up; the guitarists from Skyhooks got their idea for it after watching Simon and me on stage. They also pinched from us the notion of writing about Australian stories. Ah well, what's the old saying? 'Imitation is the sincerest form of flattery.' To go on would be to start behaving like the Nullarbor nymph.

19

The Moonbirds' first rift

One night in bed when I was cuddling into Julia's spine, I caressed a bump in her stomach. She whispered she was pregnant. I was over the moon! To think I was going to be a father!

'We're both too young,' she told me as she reached over to her bedside cabinet and found her cigarettes. 'Besides, we've got the band to think about. Don't you remember Richard's advice about appearing to be single?' Julia sat up and with trembling fingers took a deep draw on her cigarette.

I remember only too well what our dickhead of a manager told us. He said we had to pretend to our fans that we were single and therefore available. If there was any hint that any of us were involved in a relationship, it would turn them off.

'Oh, come off it, Jules! When all the Beatles got married, I didn't hear about any great decline in their record sales!' When I sat up to caress her bare shoulders, she pulled away from me.

'That's because they'd reached the stage where they didn't give a shit about the band any more!' Julia gave me one of her withering stares.

'They've all got strong solo careers. Again, I never heard of any great loss in their sales after they got married. Besides, you know and I know that Richard couldn't manage a chook raffle in a pub. Our success is due to our talent. We would have burst through no matter who our bloody manager was. Anyway, a lot of it was to do with me meeting Mike Wotzitski in the pub, not bloody Richard! He's only telling us that rubbish because while you're still single he thinks there's hope for him!'

'Bullshit, Shane!' Julia butted out her cigarette, pulled on her flannelette shirt then lit another.

'It's not bullshit, Jules. That lech has always had designs on you. Anyway, we all know he's a wanker, so why are you taking his advice? Why are you rejecting mine without giving me a chance, eh? Don't I have any say in it? After all, I'm the father. Can I have one of those?' I pointed towards her cigarettes.

She threw her packet at me. 'So much for you saying it should be a matter of choice. You're such a fucking Catholic, Shane. You know I despise anything to do with that church. They teach what I'm about to do as a sin, it's murder! You bloody Christians destroyed my great-grandmother's culture and ruined my mother's life. She was excommunicated when she married Freddie because the stupid priest said he was a heathen.' Julia turned her back on me to look out the window.

It being Brunswick, there wasn't much to look at, only a brick wall.

'"What I'm about to do". Thanks, Julia, thanks a lot. Like I say, I'm only the father. Catholic! Good on you, Julia. It just shows how much you really listen to me. I've told you heaps of times I lost my faith after getting the Christ beaten out of me and when my mum died. The last time I was in a church was at your father's funeral.' I blew my cigarette smoke up to the cracks and bugs on the ceiling. 'Don't I have any rights? Would you please listen to me?'

A snort was Julia's response, so I gave it a try. 'I love you, Jules. I adore you, I guess you feel the same way about me.'

All I got was another snort.

'I'm stoked by the news! A baby that's part of me, part of you! Let's get married, Julia.'

My lover gave a deep groan.

'We can take some time off, set up a house somewhere. After all, you were the one who told me that you're scared by the momentum the Moonbirds have created, so let's get off the roller-coaster for a while. Besides, I think we've done all we can do now.'

'Richard's got plans for us to go to England,' she said.

'England! Fucking England! The bloody graveyard of Australian bands, you mean! What about Tim Keay's advice – don't go there until you have a hit!'

'And stay here and get married. Pah! You know I hate the idea. Women are enslaved. They end up being domestic servants to you men and kids. You know I hate kids, Shane. I don't have a maternal bone in my body.'

She's not wrong there, I thought to myself. I remembered a recent party where Julia turned into an iceberg when a toddler came up to her.

'Anyway, I'm just barely managing to handle my emotions, let alone anybody else's. All women I've seen in a long-term marriage end up being miserable. Look at my mother with her face as hard as the Apostles. Shit, Shane, I'm barely coping with my life as it is now. I've just pulled myself out of a dark patch and I know I'll slip back in if I did the boring domestic thing. Can you really see us as Mr and Mrs Suburbia? It's a joke, all of it's a joke. At least with the Moonbirds there's an excitement, an uncertainty, an unknown. With marriage, I'd join the army of boring, nondescript miseries. Just look around you, Shane! You know marriage isn't for me. I'm not a part of the moronic majority.'

'Thanks a lot, Julia.' I coughed on her cigarette.

'Oh, Shaney, let's just leave things as they are now. At least we're both happy, if not… I think you're too good for me. You'd be better off with another woman. I don't think I can give you what you want.' Julia slowly shook her head.

'Like I said before, I adore you. If you don't want to listen to me, listen to Sue.'

The mention of Sue's name made her jolt. I looked up her number in Julia's pocket phone index and started to dial.

'Don't, Shane, don't. I don't want her to get involved!'

'If you can't involve your best friend, who can you involve? Hello?'

Sue's mother answered the phone.

'Hello, Mrs Sutcliffe. Is Sue there, please?'

'She's having a lie down at the moment, Shane. She's not been well, poor love. She's been suffering from some pretty bad migraines. I've been telling her to ease up on her painting but she won't listen.'

'Please, Mrs Sutcliffe, it's pretty important. Julia needs to talk to her urgently.'

'What's wrong, Shane?'

'I'd rather not say. Please, Mrs Sutcliffe!'

'All right, son, I'll go and get her.'

As I fondled the phone coil and waited for what seemed an eternity, Julia dropped her head and stared lifelessly at the mouldy carpet. If anyone could give her the right advice, it would be Sue. I remembered all those warm conversations we had after Freddie's death.

'Hello? Hello, Shane, what's up?' Sue's sleepy voice whispered down the other end of the line, hundreds of miles away at Portmagee.

I sighed as I heard the familiar sound of waves in the background.

'Please, Sue, can you talk to Julia? She needs to speak to a sane voice.'

'Me sane? Ha! OK, Shane, put her on.'

I held the phone up to Julia; she hesitated then reluctantly took it from me. I left the room to go for a walk.

I had no idea what they spoke of when I pounded through the grey backstreets of Brunswick that afternoon. It was spring, so Mother Nature hadn't made up her mind about the weather and at one stage I had to take shelter below the balcony of a milk bar as a tropical downpour lashed Blythe Street, then I had to seek the shade of an elm tree in Royal Parade because my scalp was getting sunburnt. I ended up buying a packet of cigarettes and chain-smoked in a café at Melbourne uni and watched long-haired, mostly bearded students engrossed in philosophical conversation. That was the day I started smoking. Maybe I should have listened to Dad's advice and gone to uni. They all looked so certain and devoted to a cause. They looked happy!

But Julia called them talking penises. 'Oh yes, they all have a lot of knowledge, even charm, but they're still boringly middle-class people who love the sound of their own voice and end up either as captains of industry or drop-outs who sponge on others.'

'She's not wrong,' I sighed to myself.

Thank God Sue's talking to her, I thought, good old life-affirming Sue. She still believed in God but not as he was taught by the church. The artist had a strong spirituality; she said sometimes when she was painting she felt a higher presence flow through her body which couldn't be put into words. Living on the coast, and through Julia's love, Sue was vitally aware of the majesty of nature; the ever changing sky, the call of the tides, the sacredness of the moonbirds, the way the land spoke to you if you opened yourself up. Christ, I missed Portmagee!

Like me, Sue had stopped going to church, but unlike me she still had a soft spot for the teachings of Jesus, although she'd read and agreed with the Danish philosopher, Kierkegaard, who said the Christian Church had become today what Christ opposed in his own lifetime. We two had both gone through the trauma where the all-seeing, all-knowing Jehovah of our childhood was dethroned and replaced by our own beliefs.

I remember how my now long-dead mother broke down and cried when she found out I no longer believed. Sue still had God almighty arguments with her parents and teachers. When we'd debated the issue of abortion in the past, Julia brought me around to the belief that it should be a woman's choice; Sue had argued that it was a complex issue and each case should be assessed on its merits.

I marched back to our flat desperate to hear what they'd discussed. Julia greeted me with a hug and a smile, I could tell by the relief on her face that she'd made a decision. We knocked off a bottle of her red wine and another, I fell asleep and then Richard arrived.

Julia disappeared for a week only to re-emerge in a separate bedroom in our manager's flat, where she refused to come out and talk to anyone and played Sandy Denny all the time on a portable stereo Richard had bought her. With a belly full of beer, I argued with him every night until we ended up wrestling and had to explain ourselves to the police. I told him I quit the band. When Simon found out, he did the same, but our scumbag of a manager waved our contracts in our faces. We consulted solicitors at Legal Aid who informed us that Richard Barton had us by the short and curlies.

And then Australia suddenly fell back into the Dark Ages. Gough Whitlam was sacked! The great man who'd raised our expectations and made us proud to be Australian was suddenly dismissed. When that drunken toad, Governor General Kerr, sacked our twice-elected prime minister, Steve and I were stunned and we took part in massive demonstrations in Melbourne.

Julia kept to her room. Simon stayed behind too; he reckoned all politicians were the same. The crowd's size gave us hope; all those people were voters, so surely Labor would get back into office. But Gough lost; there was a massive landslide to the Liberals and boring old plum-in-the-mouth rich cockie from our Western District, Malcolm Fraser, stormed in.

The Tories, the great upholders of the status quo, ripped up two vital conventions of our Westminster system to snatch power. The first convention was that the upper house had no right to block supply. The second, the crown was duty-bound to accept the advice of his or her minister. Imagine the uproar if the Queen sacked her government.

What really pissed me off was the media; they circled Gough's government like a shiny-toothed pack of sharks. We suffered hysterical headlines and rants from those bullet-headed Saxon mother's sons on the telly and radio on a daily basis. It was usually rubbish about financial mismanagement and who was supposedly rooting who. Who cared? Nearly all the journos revealed their true colours: beige.

The irony was that Australia, in the shadow of the international oil crisis, was about the only Western country still registering positive economic growth. The Australian historian Manning Clark believed Australian politics to be a battle between the expanders and contractors of life. In 1975, the contractors triumphed.

20

Woman of the Quiet Sun

Kensington, London. Our terrace house was a dump. The feeble sun rose, if we were lucky, at eleven in the morning, then disappeared at three in the afternoon; it was a suburb of permanent twilight. It was good to get away from the Liberal government but Simon and I rapidly became homesick and we despised this city where people judged one another by the way they dressed and spoke. But Steve, being the party animal he was, loved London and a succession of Englishwomen who found his rough colonial looks and irreverence a breath of fresh air.

Julia and Richard inhabited another dreary terrace house across the road from Kensington Park. We hardly saw them. Probably the most exciting thing for me was feeding the squirrels below Peter Pan's statue in the park.

Our manager told us he was walking through the streets of London every day to promote us. Their tatty curtains were always drawn so I assumed they were hitting the drugs again. As the gas meters clicked (what is it with the Poms and their bloody stingy meters?), our fingers turned blue and the traffic moaned, Simon and I kept churning out songs.

After the abortion, Julia no longer joined us. The only time we saw her those days was when we performed on stage together in half-empty venues dodging beer cans. Steve headbutted them back into the crowd and, hurling back abuse, he called the crowd 'limp-wristed Pommy bastards'. Simon and I were so pissed off! We'd gone from number one band in Australia to complete strangers in this permanently cold, misty, crowded city that no longer swung. The Beatles died years ago. To think that previous generations of Australians had called this dreary island home!

It was the supposed culture that got to me. My fellow countrymen tend to be open, friendly and chatty with each other ('unless you're a wog or a black fella', Steve reminded us). In London, I found I was made to feel inferior as soon as I opened my mouth. People looked down their nose at my accent. Steve said Simon and I were too serious, that all that you had to do was shit-stir the average Pom and then they'd open up to you. He was probably right.

Looking back on it now, I think a big problem was my aching yearning to return to Portmagee. I used to picture the lighthouse, East Beach, Deen Maar, the Stump Hotel all in my head in the middle of the dead meter freezing night as I watched the traffic shadows float over the flaking ceiling of our Kensington hovel.

In all the years of our touring the British Isles, the only place I felt truly at home was Ireland. Even though my family had been in Australia for five generations, as soon as the Irish heard me I was made to feel like I was one of them; of course the name McCarthy helped as well. I went back to the town of Wicklow where my ancestor Brendan was born a hundred and fifty years ago and was amazed that this seaside village was a dead ringer for Portmagee!

Unlike in England, the Moonbirds music was welcome at the Grand Hotel and when the locals joined in with us with their tin whistles, bodhráns, accordions and fiddles, I felt like I was back in the Stump. Richard and Julia had to drag me kicking and screaming back to London.

The big reason I was despondent, though, was Julia. I don't think I ever recovered from our break-up. I was down for months; I had a constant ache in the base of my gut which kept me up at night. I nearly lost it at one stage when, after months of sleeplessness, my mind became deranged and I kept heading off down to London Bridge with the idea I'd chuck myself off when nobody was around. Trouble was every time I went down there, even in the middle of the night, there were Poms everywhere.

Simon, God bless him, knew what was going on, and was always there to talk to and keep me interested in writing songs. Many's the night he suffered my drunken rantings over Julia; in his friendly non-judgemental way, he helped. Julia sometimes small-talked before we went on stage but every time I tried to approach her about our relationship, she put on the stone face she'd inherited from her mother and great-grandmother, tossed out of the waves all those years ago.

My mother Mary came to me one night as I dangled over the jaundiced waters of the fast flowing Thames. So I reluctantly kept moving. An important lesson I learnt back then was that when my mind chattered it needed to be quelled, otherwise it could kill me. Alcohol and drugs can give relief but nevertheless your anxiety will come back to haunt you in the sober light of morning.

I took up reading again and went back to all those writers Julia, Sue and I had once lovingly shared – Shakespeare, D.H. Lawrence, Hardy. I caught the bus with Simon to the Tate Gallery to rediscover William Blake. That master of heartfelt poems and dreamlike imagery became my companion as I walked through the streets of London. I saw his angels, his golden chimney sweeps, his ghosts. The meditative process of reading helped soothe my troubled brain. As my dead mother advised me, I kept composing, walked a hell of a lot and seldom brooded. Because, if you lie on your bed, darken your window and obsess over how bad life is, it's a sure-fire ticket to hell.

After about a year in London, Richard finally got us a session with a well-known record producer.

He asked us what we had and when we started to play our current crop of material, he kept interrupting us by shouting, 'Stop! That one's shit! Next!' The arrogant bastard halted us a dozen times until he heard the opening riff of a brand-new song I'd just composed called 'Woman of the Quiet Sun'. 'That's the one!' he roared.

Because we'd won Battle of the Bands back in Australia, the

Moonbirds were entitled to make a recording in Abbey Road. Simon and I knew we'd entered a sacred place. To think this was where John, Paul, George and Ringo had created their timeless masterpieces. Our eyes widened and jaws hit the floor until Steve came lumbering in with two spunky English chicks under each arm. They sat nearby with reverential looks as he produced a stubby from his duffel coat, emptied it and started to tap away on his drums. Then Julia arrived with a huge black mohair jumper like a rug, and bright pink cords. Her glazed eyes had dark circles below them. Simon and I cleared our throats and tuned our guitars, then Julia counted in and we sang, 'Woman of the Quiet Sun'. Her eyes moistened, as this was a ballad devoted to her and our past love. We cut the B-side called 'Juliette'. Like her personality, her voice was far away, sounding like it came from some distant valley. Our single hovered at the bottom of the UK charts for a few weeks then disappeared. It made it to number one in Australia and Ireland. And then suddenly, punk music exploded.

21

The house meeting

When our English manager, Malcolm McFadden, told us to get our hair cut, stop wearing make-up and toughen up our image, Julia told him to go and get fucked. We saw Johnnie Rotten on the telly being egged on to swear by that obnoxious drunken interviewer. His foul words created a huge furore in the British media, but to us Moonbirds, Johnnie's words and behavior were no different to the average gronk you encountered in a pub.

Pogo-jumping, snarling, spitting Mohawks suddenly turned up to our gigs, but Julia's angry words and Steve's size, usually kept these drop-kicks under control. The new music was a celebration of macho aggression, but when your average punk encountered an attractive and no-nonsense girl from the Antipodes, they didn't know how to react and that, combined with our long-haired larrikin drummer from the bush, stopped any Mohawk from getting his tomahawk out.

The Poms were a funny lot back then, still are, not used to showing their emotions. The punk explosion gave them the excuse to play up, but because they were so repressed it came out in extreme ways, fights and riots, whereas the Moonbirds were all Celts, and thus used to revealing how we felt usually joyous or melancholy. We didn't need a social movement or fashion to tell us how to behave. In fact, we started going the opposite way. Steve, Simon and I grew our hair longer, Julia began wearing casual clothes like red woolly jumpers, crimson chords and, with her unkempt hair, she always looked as if she'd just got out of bed, which usually was the case. Somehow our audience continued to grow.

We became good mates with our fellow Aussie band, the Saints. They were Brisbane boys who miraculously produced that great proto-punk song 'I'm Stranded' in 1976, months before the Sex Pistols blasted onto the music scene. When our countrymen were getting the same pressure from their record company to look and act more like punks, they did the same as us. They grew their hair long and decided to appear scruffy rather than designer punk. Musically like us, they were willing to take risks too, being the first new wave band to experiment with a brass section. 'Know Your Product' ranks up there with one of the best all-time Australian classics. I got shivers up and down my spine when I was in the audience to hear the Saints preview it in the technical college at Slough. Steve was there too.

We showed those Poms how to dance. None of that jumping up and down on the spot rubbish, but swaying your arms up to the ceiling, kicking your shoes off to stomp up the dust and throw your head back to harmonise with the dishevelled stars on stage. That night we got outrageously drunk with the lead singer, Chris Bailey, to celebrate his masterpiece. As far as I know, it never charted anywhere.

Whether it was due to the increased aggression of the punk audiences or the copious amount of drugs Julia and Richard were taking, Julia started arguing with us on stage. This was serious stuff, because in the past we had this unspoken rule to never get stuck into each other while we were performing.

At first it was little things. She picked on an imagined bum note one of us in the band had supposedly committed. I say imagined, because by now, with the hundreds of gigs we'd played together, the Moonbirds were a tight little outfit. She seemed to be almost willing the band on to make a mistake. We tried to laugh off her criticism, but it was now getting to the stage where she'd nitpick about nearly every bloody thing.

Of course, Richard was useless; he claimed to have heard the bum notes as well. We finally shut him up after Simon arranged a recording of one of our gigs in the Top Ran Suite in Sheffield, when we demanded that he show us our musical mistakes. Our useless bundle of poop of a manager furiously fast forwarded and reversed the cassette tape but couldn't find a bloody thing. What he did discover was an argumentative Julia unnecessarily dragging out the gaps between each song. Richard smashed the cassette player against the wall but never said anything to our lead singer.

Steve got a life-altering letter from Melbourne. Des Twentyman, one of his footy mates from Warrnambool, had made it big time by playing for the North Melbourne premiership team. He'd spoken to coach Ron Barassi, about Steve, and Des reckoned Barasi was definitely interested.

'OK, Farton, Barton, you're on notice. I'm giving you a month to sort out the Moonbird bullshit, otherwise I'm going back to Melbourne to talk to Barassi.' Steve pointed his substantial finger into the middle of Richard's pale face.

'What do you mean, man?' Our manager's clouded green eyes cleared momentarily.

'What do I fucking mean? You've gotta get her off whatever drug she's on at the moment. I don't give a rat's arse about you, but I do about Julia. Whatever you've got her on has turned her into a vegetable for starters, and she's too bloody precious these days! The Moonbirds can outplay any band on this planet, yet she's coming out about all this bollocks over our ability. It's got to stop. You're the fucking manager, so start managing, otherwise I'm going home!'

Steve emptied a long-neck beer. Home! I thought to myself, twelve thousand miles away; the other side of the world. Green and gold trams gliding along Collins Street, Flinders Street Station, the MCG, home of real football. The sun, the gloriously warm, embracing sun! The wide open plains of the Western District, the stone fences, the ocean, Sue!

'Oh, I see, man. Iit's perfectly all right to drink all day, isn't it!' Richard nodded his red cropped head at Steve.

'I'm a pisshead and I don't deny it but you're in fucking denial. At least I can still function. Churchill was a drunk, but he led Britain against

Hitler, teetotaller Hitler, that little square-mustached arsehole who never touched a drop. The world would have been better off if the great dickhead threw up in a dunny. Drunkenness makes you fallible. Anyway, I still play a mean pigskin, I can still yarn, get on with people, whereas you've turned Julia into a junkie. Get her off the crap or I go, carrot top!'

Sue sent me postcards from Melbourne. She was doing a Fine Arts degree at Melbourne Uni. The artist also sent me photos of her latest paintings, which were getting more and more abstract. Red was her favourite colour, the unique red you see in the desert country north of the Western District. I plastered her cards and pictures all over the peeling wallpaper of our Kensington flat. I'd stare at them for hours to disappear into my own red imaginary world. As another English winter approached, she sent me a letter to say how she hadn't heard from Julia for ages. I couldn't stand the thought of living in this city of perpetual twilight. But I thought of my pledge to Freddie, what seemed all those years ago, to look after his daughter.

'What do you reckon, Macca, sitting in your beanbag like a shag on a rock?' Steve suddenly asked me.

I slowly stared up at him.

'Moonface? What do you reckon?' Steve's loud voice stirred Simon from his slumber on our cat-piss-smelling couch.

'I agree with you, Steve. You've got a month, Barton, otherwise I'm knicking off back home as well.'

I rubbed the bristles on my chin.

'Moonface?' Steve ripped the lid of another longneck.

'I want to go home. I fucking hate this city, being surrounded by twelve millions Poms. It's so claustrophobic. Another cold Christmas, where you can't go for a swim, or go out and play cricket in the sun after a big meal.'

Simon kicked our clicking gas meter. It gave a slight hiss.

'I guess that settles that then. House meeting is over.' As Steve slapped Richard hard on the head, his skin cracked.

Our manager slid out of the room like a disturbed snake.

22

Back in Melbourne

Steve played in the legendary North Melbourne team of the 70s; he was in the middle of the heart-breaking grand final draw with Collingwood in 1977. I was there too; it was the first grand final draw in VFL history. Twiggy Dunne just managed to kick a goal for Collingwood before the siren blew. A hundred thousand people, including me, stood stunned below the gold September light thinking what the hell happened now?

Ah, the light! That was the first thing I noticed as we got off the jet at Tullamarine. The intense, eye-squinting light of Australia; what a contrast to the pale washed-out skies of London. At night, I rediscovered how my homeland's stars blazed like huge lanterns. What happens to a culture when they can no longer look up and revere the wonders of the night sky?

I remember Julia telling me once, as we were staring up at the Portmagee stars, that her grandmother said our ancestor's first spirituality came from the sky; from the sun, the moon, the constellations. The journeys of the heavenly bodies were the first hymns, the sacred grounds, the first altars. The ancient connection we had with the celestial spirits was being severed by neon light.

I met Sue in a café at Melbourne University, the same café I went to after the argument with Julia. She looked a lot paler, probably due to living in the city, I thought to myself, but she was over the moon to see me. I smelt the fragrance of her sea breath as she greeted me with a long silent hug. I whispered that I missed her, told her how her cards and paintings lit up the walls of our flat in Kensington and her letters always raised Simon's spirits and mine. I revealed how I thought of her when our jet soared over the vastness of central Australia for six hours.

Her faced beamed when I said that being up there, observing the red desert, the dead ancient river systems and the time-worn mountains reminded me so much of her work. She said that when she went to the Flinders Ranges with some of her fellow uni students it changed her life. Her brown eyes widened as she told me it was a completely different world up there. At night you really do sense the ancientness and remoteness of the place. Sue was fortunate enough to meet some Aboriginals who taught her that every part of the land has a story behind it. What Europeans see as a desert is, to the indigenous, a living, breathing landscape, enriched by knowledge and wisdom.

I told her of my immense relief once I'd touched the soil of my homeland. I wasn't in a hurry to go back overseas.

We went back to her flat, where we spent the afternoon drinking gallons of tea, sharing our dreams and discussing Julia. She had been as distant from Sue as she had been from the rest of the Moonbirds.

When I walked back to my uncle Brian's flat that night, I noticed billboard posters advertising Sue's up and coming exhibition at the Ian Potter Museum of Art at her university. Not bad for a kid who'd only been in town for a couple of years, I thought to myself. I laughed as a ring-tailed possum scuttled over a power line in Blythe Street.

We managed somehow to get back into Mike Wotzitski's studio to record what we thought would be our last album. Because we all felt this was to be the Moonbirds' last hurrah, there was hardly any aggro. Richard kept well away from us, thank Gough! Simon and I worked on a new batch of songs that were primarily about women whose name rhymed with Julia, for example Basia, Theresa, even Alessandra. We wrote songs about the fall of a woman, 'She's Fading', 'She's Leaving'.

Simon came up with some gems mainly to do with the landscape. 'Sunset at Fanore' was about an amazing sunset we'd observed on the west coast of Ireland, in a place called the Burren. The area is all limestone rock and when the sun plunged into the Atlantic Ocean, the light reflected on the lunar landscape around us until everything appeared as if it was on fire. It's one of Simon's best songs. He also wrote another doozy called 'Sugarloaf Mountain', which was based on his love for the Dandenong Ranges.

Julia wrote a pearler of a song called 'Our Dusk Visitor', a haunting little song about a blackbird that used to visit her childhood home at Portmagee at dusk. She also wrote some cutting songs about the uselessness of a particular male entitled 'The Slug', 'The Barwon Heads Bunyip' and 'Kerosene Jack'. She sang all of our songs with great passion, particularly the ones Simon and I had written about women. She broke down and cried when she sang my song called 'Nugget and Midge', which was about the death from old age of my two furry childhood companions. Those two little souls always picked up my mood and made it a point to sit close to me when I was ill or down. Cats are the prefect companions for the creative.

We agreed to call the album *Songs from the South-west Coast*. It went straight to number one in Australia and Ireland and peaked at number two in England, where it was just beaten off by the Clash's *Sandinista*. Oh well, if you're going to get done by a band, it might as well be by the best and, let's face it, the Clash were the best back then.

The curious thing was that our album was making waves in America. I say curious because America was shaking off the torpor of disco and was embracing new wave music. Somehow we were classified with the latter. Richard became ecstatic when our album broke into the American top one hundred. Tim Keays's advice came back into my head: never visit another country unless you've got a hit, and sort out any personality problems before you head off overseas. Well, our internal problems still simmered away, none of us liked the idea of a massive tour of the States, and was ninety-two on the charts a hit?

23

Moonshine and sorrow

The Knack's 'My Sharona' was the breakthrough song in America that swept corporate music back into the bin where it belonged. Suddenly America was full of punk, new wave bands that were singing the same stuff England had produced a couple of years earlier. But was it as simple as that?

Well…no. Your early English punk bands got their sound from America. They listened to the same musicians as the Moonbirds: the Velvet Underground, Lou Reed, John Cale, the Modern Lovers ('Pablo Picasso was never called an asshole'), Iggy Pop, the Ramones, Patti Smith and so on. Julia loved Patti Smith but I couldn't stand her. She was too hippy for me. All those Yanks pioneered the rough, ready sound which became punk. When the English bands in the 70s repeated what they'd done in the 60s, they brought rock 'n' roll back to its homeland, and the Moonbirds flew in the new music's wake. Richard made himself invisible as we did a two-month tour of America in October–November 1979.

The first thing I recall is how we were escorted everywhere. New wave bands with an outspoken female lead singer were considered controversial back then and we were always flanked by big, burly bodyguards. Then of course there was the legendary American ignorance of anything outside its borders. With our accents, we were always mistaken for being bloody English! When we'd say we were from Australia we'd always get, 'Oh yeah, that's next door to Switzerland, isn't it?'

'No, you septic tank, that's fucking Austria!' our new drummer, Alan Barr, one of Steve's drinking mates from Warrnambool, replied. Alan was an all-round barbarian, as most good drummers are.

Our album moved from ninety-two to seventy-five on the charts.

Richard occasionally booked us into venues that held thousands, but only a handful of people turned up. Sometimes we'd get booed off stage because the punters had come expecting a punk band. Sometimes the tiny crowds were great; we'd get a chance to joke, drink and laugh with them.

I hazily recall a very drunken night with some black people in Atlanta. They identified with us because Julia revealed she had Aboriginal blood in her. Some of the redneck towns were surprising too. We'd expected hostility, but because our music had a Celtic tinge to it, they loved us. It reminded them of their own bluegrass music.

I vaguely remember another terrific night after a concert in Knoxville where we got incredibly snakes-hissed with a local peach orchard farmer, Freddie, of all names, and piled into the back of his cart. His horse, without the aid of a driver, guided us through the foggy wilds of the Appalachian Mountains safely back to his farm. Ah, the Appalachians make our Dandenongs look like pimples! American trees seem to burst with life. Their rivers make ours look like creeks. The local people reminded me of the people of Portmagee.

Our album got up to number fifty in the charts.

Then there were the big trains we sat in and watched the vast landscapes slowly sail by. Julia always became animated once we got out of the big cities. The trains had names like the Zephyr or Superchief. Their engines would roar like dinosaurs as they pulled into a station and then hum as we sailed through extraordinarily rich grass plains or giant mountain ranges. The bonnets of these monsters were painted in the colours of traditional Indian headdresses. Julia and I agreed that it's in the countryside that you locate the spirit of a country. Cities tend to blur into a crowded sameness.

I remember talking with her one night as we sat high up in the Vista

Dome in one of these trains. She suddenly turned silent as the western horizon lit up. At first we thought it was a city, but then we realised we were witnessing the rise of the full moon over the great plains of America. It was bloated and rose up in the sky like the face of all-seeing God.

When I saw the trace of a tear in my ex-lover's eyes, my heart expanded. There was no need for words. We both knew we were sharing a golden embrace from something greater than our earthly concerns. I went downstairs to pull a bottle of white wine from under the bed in my sleeper.

She uttered, 'God bless you,' as I poured her a glass.

The air was fragrant with the smell of grass. We knocked the bottle off then lounged back in our seats. Julia and I were one, and our carriage became luminous. I found my guitar and started strumming, she hummed and we composed until the early hours of the morning what would turn out to be the Moonbirds' greatest songs.

****

Richard raced us into the RCA studios in New York, where we cut the album simply entitled *The Moonbirds*. It was straight-from-the-heart music backed up by a hefty dose of inspiration from the moon, wine and a love for the land. It was our most acoustic and folksy album and hence flew in the face of what was going on around us. It turned out to be our last, because of Krauss Stifter.

As we were recording, Julia received a small book in our Bank Street apartment called *Conceive This*, by Krauss Stifter. It was full of Krauss's paintings and photos accompanied by the words 'conceive this'. Krauss penciled in a thought with every image. For example, he'd painted a bird with a seed in its mouth flying below a rainbow and wrote, 'Conceive this, the flood shall return.' Another page had a picture of a white cloud with 'Conceive this, there are no boundaries in the sky.' Then another page presented a diving stuka, with 'Conceive this, a bomb exploding with love', and so on.

'Hippy shit!' was our drummer's reaction.

Yet Julia kept flicking though the pages with a big smile on her face as she lounged on her double bed in the back room. New York light filtered through a skylight to give her the appearance of a reclining marble statue.

One night when our bodyguards were ordering burgers across the street, a gaunt-looking guy stepped out of the shadows to ask, 'Ms King?'

'Yeah, who's asking?' replied our lead singer.

'I'm Krauss Stifter. Vat did you think of my book?' He had long frizzy hair and an axe murderer look.

'Oh, it's you! I think it's beautiful.'

Julia's chest heaved, Krauss's rigid body melted and before we knew it, he was in our apartment expanding upon his book. We were all knackered from a long day of recording but subjected to a long lecture on the virtues of his brand of existentialism.

Like most New Yorkers I'd met, he was intense, yet Julia said she loved that quality in the people, their upfront attitude meaning that they had no time for the niceties of life and just got on with it. After a while, our drummer collapsed on the huge earth-brown velvet sofa with a bottle of beer and put the big colour telly on. Although Simon and I complained about the weak as piss quality of American beer, we pulled bottles out of the green fridge and joined our drummer.

Julia and Krauss continued their conversation, which was more like a rant from this German American. At about midnight, Richard stuck his head briefly through our door and gave out a long sigh before he floated back to his separate apartment. Hand in hand, Julia and Krauss went off to the back room with the skylight.

Thank God we'd almost finished making our album, because Julia broke another cardinal rule of the band by allowing Krauss to come into the recording studio. That had never happened before! It was bad enough putting up with his constant presence but then he started making suggestions on how we could improve our music!

'Vhy don't you try zis? Vhy don't you try zat?' Krauss demanded with a crazed gleam in his Teutonic eye.

Simon and I were too stunned to reply.

'Why don't you get fucked, you useless kraut!' Praise the lord for our drummer!

Oh no! I thought to myself as Alan and Krauss started chesting each other. She's chosen another alpha male. What is it about intelligent women and alpha males? Why do they go for these opinionated baboons?

Simon separated the roosters.

One night there was a loud rap on our hotel door.

'Hey, guys, I'm the house dick!' A dark-looking little Italian American, with a big ring of rattling keys and a droopy moustache, burst into our room. 'Hey, do any of you Auzzies know the big bozo down the hall?'

'Yeah, he's our so-called manager. Why?' I asked.

'Well, because he's as dead as a dodo. Whatdya know about that?' The house dick lit up a cigar.

The walls were made of dark wood. His clothes were tossed over a white shag pile rug. A red lava lamp splodged away in the corner of the room, the ash tray was a mountain of butts and bottles of various shapes and forms littered the floor. His tall plank of a body was still warm. Julia was convinced all she had to do was give his shoulders a firm shake; but there was no response. And then there was that grimace on his face. Something painful had passed through his troubled brain. What happened in those last fleeting moment? Did he take the hurt with him to the otherworld or was it extinguished by death's lonesome embrace?

Julia wept, so did I. Krauss kept crapping on about 'Vel, I didn't know za guy so it's of no concern to me,' before Alan told him to fuck off.

Songs from the South-west Coast, hovered at number-fifty in the US then our new album, *The Moonbirds*, became an international smash hit! Two songs from the new album, 'Albert Street' and 'The Sailor's Daughter', made it into the top ten practically everywhere. Richard's instincts were right after all. Krauss wrote an article about Richard's death which was published in *Rolling Stone*.

It created a controversy after Julia was quoted as saying, 'Christianity's just a myth. Why it got chosen as the supposed truth out of all the other myths at the same time, Roman, Greek, Egyptian, Celtic and so onc, is beyond me. Richard soul's will be nursed by Bundjel. He's the creator spirit of our land, not bloody Jesus, for God's sake!'

Simon and I flew back across the Pacific with Richard's body and then we accompanied him down to Geelong in a hearse for the funeral. Death makes a companion of us all, someone said, and I thought about that as I stared at the pyramid shapes of the You Yangs. Julia, Krauss and Alan stayed in New York.

To this day, there's still a mystery how Richard Barton died. He had sleeping problems and swallowed nearly a bottle full of sleeping tablets which, combined with a sea of whisky, became a lethal cocktail. But whether it was deliberate or not, nobody knows. Still, I'll never forget that look on his face when he saw Julia and Krauss's banging on that night.

Looking back on it now, it seems a classic case of depression. He felt he never met the expectations of the people close to him and he gave up once he saw Julia was attracted to Krauss. Or maybe he was so out of his brain he didn't know what he was doing? Who the hell knows? We humans are such complex creatures. Poor young Richard; silly bugger.

24

A tale of two villages

Months later, we got a letter from Julia in her handwriting, but the tone revealed Krauss as its author. It was rude, aggressive, basically declaring Krauss was the new manager, and demanding that if we didn't return to the States within a week of receipt, we would be sacked from the Moonbirds. Simon and I used the letter for mulch.

A month later, we burnt an identical letter on the hearth. Our album remained number one in the charts for months at the beginning of the new decade; the media speculated that we'd broken up. Krauss, Julia and Alan hosed down any suggestions of our demise. Simon and I moved back down to Portmagee in the spring of 1980 and we refused to talk to any bloodsucking leech of a reporter. I've hated them since 1975.

We'd purchased an old bluestone whaler's cottage called Cooinda over the hill from East Beach. When the weather was good, Simon and I sat out on the front veranda, yarned, smoked and listened to the ocean.

Cooinda's tin roof made us aware of the rain that bucketed down practically every night then cleared the next morning. The sky was always moving, usually a storm which was swept away by a starling-chiming blue sky. We bought two tortoiseshell cats and named them Christy after the legendary Irish folk singer Christy Moore, and Minnaloushi after the cat in the Yeats poem 'The Cat and the Moon'.

Portmagee old-timers told us the reason Cooinda was so cheap was because it was haunted. Apparently its builder Lloyd Rutledge was fond of the good stuff and after one heavy night on the turps fell down the stairs and broke his neck. There was a huge storm the day of his burial. The thunder and lightning spooked the horses so they couldn't put poor old Lloyd into the hearse and had to carry him physically all the way to the Portmagee cemetery. When they lowered him down to his grave, the rope slipped and he fell down head first.

Down here, where lightning hisses around the surrounding empty paddocks and our windows and doors rattle after each thunderclap, it's no wonder Portmagee produces such stories. But to be honest, Simon and I never came across old Lloyd's ghost, although Sue reckoned otherwise when she saw him smiling at her one night at the base of the stairs as we chatted around the open fire. He was smoking a pipe, wearing a vest and donning heavy cloth trousers.

Sitting around and talking was what we did a lot of those days. Richard had failed to negotiate a deal that we had to produce records within a certain time frame, so we were under no pressure to set to work on another album.

I rediscovered the preciousness of my friendship with Simon. We bludged gloriously now that we were away from the madness of touring and performing. Good old Moonface: what a great mate he'd always been. We never argued and we laughed a lot. As you can tell from this writing, I often take myself too seriously. Simon's always had a wonderful ability to pull my plug whenever I become pompous.

We grew our own dope plants amongst the tomatoes in our vegie patch. Harvest time was a lot of fun. We choofed heaps, wrote some good stuff the next day, and had a regular Friday night gig at the Stump. The pub was always chockers; people came from all around Australia and the world to see us. Simon laughed but I got pissed off when he read a review about us in *The Sun*. The reporter hinted that we were gay. I wondered if Krauss was behind it.

The Moonbirds lived on in New York. Julia adored Soho's nineteenth-century cobbled streets and warehouses; they reminded her of Portmagee. She loved the noisy markets of Chinatown, the out-there galleries, the always open bars (frequented by our drummer who said it was the only way he could tolerate Krauss), and the unique boutiques. The city was full of eccentric people who took creativity seriously and everybody seemed to know everybody, so that it was like living in a giant village.

Then, of course, there was the harbour, and Krauss. Julia being such an intense person, it made sense where she ended up. Australia tends to be scornful of people who stick out from the crowd, especially if you're a woman. She resided in a city with a long and proud history of promoting the arts. She had a partner who appeared interested in experimenting with ideas, although like all artists it was on his terms. We kept getting legalistic letters from America that made good fire starters. Julia and Krauss found an apartment and they asked a couple of Krauss's drinking buddies to join the band.

When Julia released a single and an album called *Conceive This*, I saw her in a film clip on *Countdown*. She'd cut off all her long beautiful hair, dressed in tight denim and seemed wistful. There was boring old 'grouse Krauss' (as Simon called him) in the background playing bass guitar with a beard and long hair. The dishevelled Nordic-looking nonentities in the background playing keyboards were the two guys who'd replaced us. Alan Barr had grown his long dark hair down to his backside and he leered at the camera every time it approached his loony face. The song, a joint ballad by Krauss and Julia, wasn't half bad; it appealed to the fans' imagination and contemplated a better world. The rest of the album was very industrial and funky, with lots of keyboards and synthesisers. Grouse Krauss had managed to scour any folk remnant from the Moonbird's sound.

I'd be lying if I said we didn't compete. Simon and I called ourselves the Shearwaters after experiencing a cloud of them over Griffith Isle at dusk. Watching the sky brim full of the silent, swooping birds is always a spiritual experience. Steve, who was getting too old for footy by this stage, rejoined us. We toured the Western District and Melbourne, and then released a new album for which Sue painted the cover. We were soon flying up the Australian charts.

The Moonbirds also released an album which took off all around the world. We'd never admit that we were listening to each other's music. Julia wrote a couple of bitchy and angry songs about me, called 'No brain Shane' and 'Portmagay guys'. Simon and I wrote a song called 'Adolph and Eva', then another 'Blitz Bitch'. Because we were firmly ensconced back in Portmagee and smoking lots of ganja, the Shearwaters weren't interested in doing another international tour. Our slothfulness baffled Julia and Krauss, for they were expecting a full-on invasion of America from the Shearwaters. It never came.

25

Good advice

Because we'd been friends for a decade, Sue and I assumed it would always be that way. She'd finished her course at Melbourne Uni and, mainly due to her headaches, came back to Portmagee to live with her parents. She'd had every test under the sun but they couldn't find anything wrong. Sue kept painting, and slowly but surely her works started selling well in Melbourne. Despite Lloyd Rutledge's ghost, she came to Cooinda every Saturday night. It was her only social event; she didn't go to the Stump on Friday nights because of the crowds. We'd get a fire going, light up a few innocent fellows, turn the lights off, drink gallons of tea and then chat about Julia and our dreams until the early hours of the morning.

Neither of us had heard from our ex-lead singer for a long time. I sat in my rocking chair while Sue and Simon lounged on the blue tartan couch. Pea Soup Beach hissed like a giant serpent. The sweet smell of plum wood wafted through the room. The clouds raced below the stars every time I went outside for a pee.

'I'm starting to think of what a waste of time it's all been, Sue.' I took a few puffs of the joint then handed it over to a nodding Simon. 'I mean, think of all the time and energy we've put into our music and what's it all been for, eh?'

'Don't say that, Shane.' Sue stroked a purring Christy on her lap. 'You know it'd be a poorer world if we didn't listen to what our hearts tell us.' She scratched the cat behind her ears. 'This world's full of deniers, miserable people, whose existence consists of trying to drag everyone else down to their boring cynical level, making everything seem bleak and superficial. Moonface, you're taking your heels with that innocent fellow.' Sue held her pale hand up to Simon and twitched her fingers.

'Oops sorry, Sue, old girl! Ah! 1980's a jolly good year, I must say. A fine vintage, what?' Simon coughed, then handed the joint to her.

'That's all right, Mooney.' Sue chuckled as she took a long draw. Christy stuck her head up and sniffed. 'Oh look, the puddy tat's getting stoned as well.'

We all cracked up.

'No, seriously, Shane…there's that moment when my painting connects with the viewer. I can see it in their eyes – for one tiny moment in time we're one and we share this attachment straight from the heart.' Sue patted her small chest. 'That moment of understanding which is beyond words, thoughts, culture, religion…it's eternal, you're lifted to a better realm. Here you go, Shane. It'll make a man out of you.' Sue passed the joint to me; her smile was as wide as the Milky Way over Bass Strait. 'I'm not boring you, am I?'

'Pah!' I drew the smoke into my chest then sighed. 'What do you mean by the eternal?'

Minnaloushi meowed as she came into the lounge room. I raised myself slowly to stoke the fire and sparks rocketed up the chimney.

'Well, existence beyond death, creation of life that defies time: children, songs, stories, paintings. They're all messages in a bottle, which live on long after we've turned to dust and hopefully go towards helping to explain what life's all about. The key to getting there is a heartfelt emotion that we all share.'

When Sue rubbed my kneecap as I sat back down on the rocking chair, her touch surged through me like a tide. Minnaloushi gave a small chirrup as she pounced onto my lap.

'The important thing, Shane, is don't become jaded. The world's full of misery guts. It's too easy to become disillusioned, not to mention bloody selfish. It's too easy… Shane, you're dragging your heels with that joint. C'mon, give it back to us, will you?'

The flames reflected in her happy gleam. Minnaloushi kneaded away on my thighs.

'If you're pissed off, why not have a break? You and Simon have been on the road for over a score of years. Why not write songs for other people? Why not write poetry?'

The plum log crackled as its sap flowed into the flames.

It was good advice. Simon and I had a trunk full of songs which we readily gave to other struggling local acts. Our songs, off and on for the next ten years, made it into the top forty. We had a smash number one hit with 'Julie, Parts 1, 2 and 3'. Despite whinges from some DJs that the song went for over ten minutes, our fans demanded that it be played in its entirety. With its pleading vocals and chainsaw guitars, it stayed at the top for six months and even created a few ripples overseas. It was a top ten hit in New York, where Krauss and Julia bought out a new album that was universally panned by the critics and didn't sell; it was a double, very political, disc called *Springtime in New York* city that sank the slipper into Ronald Reagan and went down like a lead balloon. Julia's songs were naïve and too full of simplistic slogans; Krauss was so far up himself that there was no way his songs about the common man could ring true. Besides, he came from a comfortable family who employed servants and nannies. What the hell would he know about a factory worker?

***

Tucked away beneath excited columns shouting about Bob Hawke's victory, was an article announcing the final break-up of the Moonbirds. I read with wide-eyed amazement the story of Julia being kicked out of her New York apartment by Krauss. How was that possible? I mean, Julia, being the main breadwinner, presumably the lease was in her name? Or even if it was a joint lease, what power did Krauss have to evict her? It didn't make sense. Or did the useless parasite have everything in his name? Now, that did make sense. Julia didn't have a practical bone in her body.

The next thing I heard, she was hosting wild parties in Los Angeles. I tried to ring her a few times but never got through. I sent her letters, Sue sent her letters, but she never answered them.

'Come home, Julia!' I shouted to her one night out on Griffith Island, on my side of the Pacific. Some fishermen shook their heads at me. While half of Australia celebrated the election of a new Labor government, I chain-smoked and pleaded to a God I didn't believe in to deliver Julia back into my arms.

26

Gale-force wind

It was the season of racing silver clouds, white sun and open fires. Smoke was whisked from Portmagee chimneys up into the maddened claws of the southern wind. Our roof threatened to blow off in the constant tumult of gale-force winds. Pea Soup Beach roared like an artillery barrage and the cats chased wind devils around our backyard. It was the time of year when any Portmagee resident who tottered on insanity plunged. Some blame the lack of sun; I believe it's the never-ceasing Antarctic winds. They make you restless, keep you awake, eat away your sanity, until you obsess about everything outside of your control.

News reporters bleated that Julia was losing the plot. She was tossed out of nightclubs, her parties raged forever and she was prone to making inappropriate statements when being circled by the microphone-wielding vultures. The cameras captured her wild-eyed look as she ranted.

'Shut up, woman!' I'd shout to the telly sometimes when she appeared.

Her ravings were about chauvinism (we men are a pack of bastards, no doubt there), the capitalist system (yes, it can be an oppressive, no doubt there either, Julia), the shitty music scene (hey, it's the 80s, she's right there too!), religion (woman, you're living in a country full of god-botherers), then what an arsehole Krauss was (well, I'm a hundred per cent behind you there too, Julia). In my bedroom wardrobe, I've got scrapbooks full of her words. Here's a small example, from an interview with *Juke* magazine:

'You men, who run the institutions that dominate us, you haven't changed one bit. Some people think we've evolved from our hunter gatherer past, you know, where the men hunted all day and the women stayed home to gather herbs and look after the children. Bloody bullshit! Every position of power is still controlled by men, the government, the banks, the fucking media, the army etc.'

'What about Margaret Thatcher?'

'Don't get me started. She's a woman with balls. She plays it by the boy's rules. She believes got to act tough. The Falkland War, what a crock of bullshit that was. I mean the old cow was rock bottom in the polls, she was going to lose the election, then all of a sudden she chose to fight over a shitty wind-swept sheep paddock in the South Atlantic. It was so bloody obvious what she was doing. All conservatives do it. Get a war going to distract the masses from the important things like unemployment and rising prices. As Sam Johnson said, "Patriotism is the last refuge of the scoundrel". Practically every time a conservative senses they're losing power they pick a fight. It's so childish; she's pathetic, she's no different, in fact she's worse than a male because she sees the need to act tough all the fucking time!.'

'Well, how else do you gain power to presumably change things for the better?'

'Women, people, shouldn't be obsessed with gaining power. There's an alternative. We all have alternatives…mine's creative… in my own clumsy way I've learnt there's a different road to the protestant work ethic. Now that I've been chewed up and spat out by the system, I don't care about it any more. There are other ways; remain true to yourself, pursue your passion, your love. Drop out of the nine-to-five. You don't need big houses, big cars, big partners, big children; big deal!

'It's the dreamers who make a difference, people who opt out. Some of us are writers, poets, songwriters, artists – hello, Sue! Others attempt to opt out and quietly build their own paradise. It's not about climbing up the ladder but throwing it on the rubbish heap where it belongs. True change comes from revolution, not political revolution, but an inner revolution of the head, a rejection of aggression, ignorance, hatred or any other negative trait you care to mention. It comes from stepping outside of the rigmarole. Toss away the way you were brought up.

'I hope my own feeble efforts, my songs, my stories, will be remembered long after I die. That's all I care about. A little piece of me will be remembered, a ripple. It has nothing to do with the acquisition of power. Most people realise that their life's been an illusion after they retire, but by then it's too late. Retire now while you've still got the energy.'

'So what you're saying is that it's all right to drop out and take drugs?'

'Like all you bloody journalists, you just don't listen do you? The demons I've fought over the years have changed me, given me insight, something you'd know nothing about you clown!'

When Julia's hot, she's hot; it's just that I worry when she says things like 'God is a fraud. I mean, where the hell is he when you really need him? If you believe the Old Testament, he was always around, a burning bush, a giant arm scribbling on a wall, a god who kept the sun up in the sky so his followers could massacre their enemies, for fuck sake, a god who pulverised sinful cities etc. etc. Now we're on the brink of nuclear and environmental disaster, where is that noisy, meddling old bloody fool when you need him? How come he's suddenly disappeared? Because he wasn't there in the first place or he's lost hope and pissed off to another planet.'

Julia's saying this in a nation that burnt Beatles records and books, recently strung black people up in trees; killed John Lennon. While her anger was justified, she's saying this where psychotics can easily get their hands on a gun. There's that sinister underside to America which Julia in her innocence overlooked.

Most Yanks I met on our tour were incredibly open, friendly and generous, but some of them also loved the sound of their own voice and seemed determined to give you their opinion even when you didn't ask for it. It can be a manic nation; there's that unspoken anger you'd see in some of their faces if you disagreed with them.

For a democratic people, some of them can be intolerant of oppositional views, which they try to shout or shoot down. But then Simon, usually with an innocent fellow dangling out of his lips, told me I worried too much and said America has a great tradition of freedom and tolerance: look at the way they humbled Nixon. Besides, my good friend argued, Julia was too big for Australia.

She went on to make her last great album in Los Angeles, *Gale-force Wind*. It was beautiful stuff. Because she was now fending for herself while experiencing life on the edge, all the superficial things were swept away and she sang straight from her soul. The music was melodic; she used plenty of acoustic guitars, fiddles, penny whistles, piano accordions, even a didgeridoo. Her voice wailed and chanted, just like her ancestors. Simon, Sue and I got shivers up and down our spine every time we played it at Cooinda.

Julia had been away for over a decade, yet her music sprang from the land and ocean around us. The songs were full of spirits: her family tossed onto the shore, the dead musicians from the now burnt-down dance hall on the outskirts of town, her father Freddie, her pained and beautiful childhood, her true friends and lovers, but it was also more.

She had somehow managed to capture the various songs of the wind, the sigh of the earth, the breath of the ocean, then merge all of these elements with a non-judgemental love. You felt like you were being serenaded by a goddess. She'd reached a stage in her life where she could shine down on the rest of us.

Despite her not touring, the album got to number one all around the world. She made a surprise appearance with Men at Work at Madison Square Garden and stole the show. She didn't know Krauss was in the audience. They saw each other for the first time in eighteen months after her performance. Julia moved back into their New York apartment. 'Our break up didn't work,' she told Juke. She soon found herself pregnant, but decided to keep the baby this time and then she vanished into the ether.

27

Return of the native

When our music waned at the end of the 80s, I branched out into poems. Most of them were dope-inspired tomes that went for pages. Sue read them and told me they were too obscure, and she was right. It was the ones I wrote on the side, without the help of drugs (except a drink or two), small nuggets about life and the Portmagee seascape, that got published. There's no money in poetry, as the old saying goes (Robert Graves says there's no poetry in money). The most I ever made from a poem was nine quid. Now I'm trying to write prose.

Simon and I toured the Western District and Melbourne whenever the bank threatened to take over Cooinda. Simon brought in a bit of dosh by becoming a record producer. If you read the album sleeves of most of the good stuff that's coming out of Australia now, you'll find he's the producer.

Sue's paintings sold all over Australia, then she started making inroads overseas. Apparently, Julia had them all over her apartment. Steve still toured with us, but moved to Melbourne to become a plumber. To this day, if you go out to the Greenwood Avenue Oval in Ringwood on a freezing Melbourne winter's morning, and see a tall giant of a man with black curly shoulder-length hair, wearing overalls, carrying a six-pack in a plastic bag and shouting out orders, it's Steve. He's coach of the Under 12s Ringwood Jets.

One night at the Caledonian there was a bloke who kept shouting badly along to our lyrics. I looked across the sea of audience heads to spy Alan Barr with his mad gleaming dark brown eyes sitting on a stool holding up the bar. He held his beer up to me every time I made eye contact with him. I meandered through the seething crowd after our first break. People kept slapping my back and asking for an autograph.

'Barr boy, you old bastard. How are you?' I shook his hand.

'On the dole, man. You want a pot, Macca?'

'Does a polar bear shit on the tundra? What are you doing back here, you old bugger?'

'Well, there's nothing left for me in the States. I've just been turfed out of another band because I decked the lead singer. Bloody septics, they're so full of themselves.' With a crinkled brow and a fag hanging out of his mouth, Alan handed me a beer.

I sculled it as the crowd chanted for us to come back.

'Listen, Barr boy!' I shouted into his ear. 'You've got to come back to Cooinda after the gig and tell us everything. I'd love to catch up with you.'

'No worries, man! It'll be a gas.'

My scalp was tense as I whispered to Simon that Barr boy was back. We raced through the set. I was dying to know the latest about Julia; we hadn't heard anything from her for ages.

'I used to be their drummer. One at a time, girls, one at a time,' shouted Barr boy to every attractive female who came within his orbit.

Simon and I did two encores, smiled, waved to a nearly out of control crowd, snatched a complaining Barr boy off his stool, then made our way through the drizzle to Sue's folks' place in Grant Street.

'What the fuck are you doing, man? You dragged me away from Helen Martin. She's the hottest chick in the whole Western District, man. She bangs like a dunny door.'

'Shoosh.'

I sneaked along the Sutcliffe's driveway, stumbled through some bushes in their back garden, found some pebbles then flicked them at the dormer window of Sue's attic. We four were soon huddled around a big fire in Cooinda.

'She's got two kids now – Sean who's about five, and Sue who's three, I think. Wee, this is good ganja, man.'

Sue and I chortled over the names of the kids.

'Helen Martin…you arseholes took her away from me, man! With her curly blonde hair and enormous norges, I reckon she's got the horns for me something fierce.' Alan sighed as he took a deep draw of the joint. 'Yeah, they're great ankle-biters. Sean's got fair hair, not like his stupid father. He's a musician already and walks around the house strumming his ukulele. Julia always has music going in the apartment, classical stuff like the Beatles, the Small Faces, Daddy Cool, Skyhooks, Bowie, Sandy Denny, Christy Moore, all the greats, even Mozart. She takes him to mini maestros and he's writing his own songs already in an exercise book. Jesus, this is good stuff, man, not like that New York shit.'

'It's home-grown, man. Here, pass it to us. Cooinda 1989's a good vintage,' Simon's moon face beamed as he puffed away on the innocent fellow.

'Sue… Ha! Sue, she's red-haired and feisty, a handful just like her mother.' Alan slowly shook his head. 'She's got this furry possum hand puppet instead of a teddy. Julia ordered it from Melbourne. She's a hands-on mother. She reckons if you're gonna have kids you should be there for them, not dump them in a crèche or have a nanny. You can tell she's doing the right thing. The kids are happy, they love a good natter and they're curious, not like those surly shits who spend most of their waking hours with strangers. Fucking New York's full of them, man. They're breeding a whole new generation of kids that never see their parents! It's dangerous stuff, man!'

'So what does she do apart from looking after the billy lids?' Simon asked as he passed the joint on to me.

'Well, that's it, man, that's all she does, be with the kids. She cooks heaps, makes her own bread and stuff now, cleans, reads to them a lot. She reads your poetry by the way, Shane. She loves it. She sings, she sings heaps to the kids. It's a fucking perfect existence, man. I want to do the same. I'm sick of being a gypsy. I wanna stay home and raise a tribe of kids. I wonder if Helen would be interested? Hmm, I mean, she's getting on a bit now.' Alan shot the joint an expectant look.

My heart beat fast with the knowledge that Julia loved my poetry. The dope took effect as I took forever to get off my rocking chair to hand him the innocent fellow.

'Is she writing any music?' asked Sue, who sat on the couch next to Simon. Her eyes drooped while a content Minnaloushi purred on her lap.

'She reckons she doesn't write any more. She hasn't showed me anything and she keeps telling me she's glad to be off the merry-go-round. I've got a suspicion she still does do it now and then, but doesn't show anyone, especially grouse Krauss. She's probably tucked her songs away in a drawer somewhere. But who knows, man? She never had a family, now she's made her own.' Alan gave a huge yawn.

'How's things with Krauss?' I lit another joint and handed it to a smiling Sue.

'You never see the arsehole. He's turned into a ghost.'

'What do you mean?' I barked out.

'Well, the arsehole is their "business manager". Yawn! Julia made a fortune out of *Gale-force Wind*. He's got a separate office that he goes to everyday where he supposedly manages their money, then he comes home and watches the telly when they have a meal. The telly's on all the time in their joint. Julia always lights up if there's anything from Oz. Then he disappears into his own separate room at night in the apartment with a computer. She hardly ever sees him and when he's around he's always a cranky old arsehole with the kids, always shouting. He scares the daylights out of them sometimes. He never says boo to me. which suits me right down to the ground. Why doesn't she just leave the arsehole? I hit the terps with her one night when the kids were in bed and Krauss was wanking himself in his own room. I saw a different Julia – she started moaning and telling me how lonely she was. I got an agreement out of her that night. She said she and the kids would come back to Portmagee. She sobbed as she hugged me. I was rapt! Our beautiful girl was finally coming home. But the next morning when I reminded her of what we'd talked about, she said it was the booze talking and there was no way she would leave New York. Fuck it!' Alan stared at the flickering shadows on the floor.

Stars were smothered by racing clouds as I smoked out on the front veranda. The ocean whispered and lightning hissed over Bass Strait. My exhausted brain didn't know what to think. Julia's not writing any more, she loves reading my stuff, she's a good mum, yet she's got this German albatross hanging around her neck. I thought of those glorious days we shared back in Brunswick. Surely they could be recreated? I'd gladly love to be a father to Sean and little Sue. With the name of her son and her following of my writing, there was a residue of love still there for me. What's the problem? Why doesn't she pack her bags and come home? Barr boy says she's a good actress. But don't we all appear that way? We put on a daylight happiness and indicate to the rest of the world we're doing fine, but when the sun goes down, we go to bed, and even if it's a double bed, we face the night alone.

Cooinda's front door creaked, a shadow floated through the doorway towards me, a cold hand brushed my hair, a soft voice told me to stop thinking and come back inside.

28

Music of the spheres

The blue water turned grey and she observed the dark clouds gathering on the horizon. The waves turned huge. Before she knew it, the yacht was plunged into a canyon of water only to be clutched by another monster wave which threw her up into the purple sky, then tossed her down into another gurgling void of black water. One by one, the crew surrendered, crippled by seasickness and the captain ordered her to take over the wheel. She argued, shouting that her tiny hands were made to play guitar, not to steer a ship.

But the exhausted captain, now reeling in pain, bellowed out the course then disappeared down into the galley. She was alone, terrified, the spray smashing against her face. Yet she understood the orders. She'd spent summers with Sean in a fourteen-foot sailing boat in Cold Springs Harbour. How was it that the crew were all paralysed in their bunks below while she was still standing?

The boat heaved and circled. 'If I can survive cold turkey from heroin, I can weather anything,' she laughed to herself. 'I've taught my body never to be sick again.'

The mainsail ripped.

'Freddie! Dad! Help me! It's your daughter, the daughter of a sailor!' she screamed out over the forty-foot waves, her voice taken by the sixty-five-mile-per-hour winds. Julia pictured her grandmother, the original Eve, and her great-grandmother, naked, weeping, spat out by a merciless ocean. She started singing the sea shanties she'd learnt as a little girl at Portmagee – folk songs, dirges, voices from the first day.

She grinned as she held her face up to the enraged sky. She heard the groan of the forty-three-foot-long yacht as it responded finally to her touch. The captain found her in the calm red wine waters of dawn, steering with the Easter Island face of the Douglas girls.

When Julia met up with the kids in Bermuda, she helped build sandcastles, walls and moats, bathed like a mermaid in the warm rock pools and taught them how to read the waves. She saw the horror in her daughter's face when she was dunked for the first time and the fear in her son's eyes as the shadows swirled below the shallows. Yet how the children slept inside their sun-kissed skins.

She dreamt of barely keeping a saloon door closed with both arms against a howling darkness. Sometimes she was captivated by the whir of a bagpipes drifting through the ever blue sky from a neighbouring property. The man was practising for the local New Year's bash. She sent him a letter of thanks and a bottle of Chivas Regal malt whisky. She bought a cassette player and tapes and after a gap of two-and-a-half years the music returned to every fibre in her body. She settled the kids, then sat out on the balcony with her guitar and laid down a few demos while the cicadas hummed and tree frogs whistled.

A rumour spread through the media that Julia was planning to visit Australia. Multimillionaire Herbert Gridlock offered two million dollars in his newspaper if the Moonbirds reunited. Simon rang Julia's number in New York and left a multitude of messages on her answering machine. She saw the silent red flashing light of the separate telephone in her white room overlooking Central Park, but she never picked it up, especially when she was composing, leaving it to Krauss instead, who'd come home from his office and delete messages he didn't like. Simon managed to get on to him once, but when Krauss waffled on about him being the manager, our bass guitarist threw the phone down.

Sue and I sent letters to her, but she didn't respond. Once we realised that Krauss would never back down from his insistence that he was to be the manager, we gave up. Besides, we hadn't played together for close to ten years. Who wanted to see a pack of geriatrics get up on stage? A whole new generation of kids had grown up since the Moonbirds imploded.

Julia's voice was on the radio again. She had a single out called 'New Beginning' and it wasn't half-bad, being a direct throwback to 50s doo wop music, the sort of schmaltzy stuff our parents used to listen to when they were kids. Suddenly she was all over the media again. She gave out interviews to *Rolling Stone*, *Playboy*, *Ram*, *Juke* and practically every other rock magazine in existence.

Here's a small example from my scrapbook:

Hello, everyone. Well we've all made it through another decade! God, the eighties were so boring? Weren't they? Love to all my family, my good friends both here in New York and Australia, I'm back brimming with ideas and songs. My kids are at school and kinder now, so I've got a bit of time to myself, and now I'm pushing forty I've learnt you've got to use every minute, every hour of waking to pursue your true love in life. Hell my life's half over now! I've been so fortunate. Out in the middle of the ocean I heard the music of the spheres and when I was playing with my children on the shoreline my muse returned, I'm so excited, I want to share my joy with the rest of you.

***

The fat loser lived in that twilight zone in which all no-hopers exist, a delusional world where their outlook on life is the only thing that matters. Not moderated by discussion or knowledge, their thoughts flush like gutter water into a drain. Their existence is isolated and bleak and the tragedy is that they see the need to inflict their soullessness on everybody else. And because they know they're failures, bloody nothings, they have a messianic sickness to go down in history. So the more cowardly of them murder the dreamers, the ones who dare to imagine that they can make it a better world. The fat loser, like all losers, had a gun. Guns don't kill people, people do with guns. I don't want to talk too much about the scumbag, because that's what he wants, attention.

The phone kept ringing in Cooinda. We didn't hear it because we hated the damn thing and kept it in a closet under the stairs.

Then Alan Barr banged on our front door. 'Shane, Simon, Sue! Wake up! Julia's been shot!'

Sue shook my chest; I fell out of our bed and staggered down the stairs. A gust of Antarctic wind hit me as I opened the door. Barr boy charged past me and put CNN on the telly, where a reporter ranted out the front of Julia's apartment. She'd been shot in the chest by a so-called fan.

Simon and Sue raced down the stairs. We were all too stunned for words. Our phone kept ringing in the closet but we ignored it. A crowd had gathered around her apartment. Then came the announcement that Julia had arrived dead on arrival at the Roosevelt Hospital. The fat loser had called, 'Ms King,' pulled out a .38 handgun, then knelt into the two-handed combat stance you see on crappy cop shows and useless computer games and fired five shots.

Julia managed to stumble up the front stairs to the main entrance, then she collapsed in the lobby. She dropped an armful of cassette tapes, which scattered all over the floor. A porter rang the alarm and attempted to apply a tourniquet to Julia's chest wounds but it was too late. He gently removed her dark sunglasses then placed his jacket over her body.

They found the fat loser nearby, leaning against a wall, reading *Catcher in the Rye*. Apparently he'd written some piss-weak statement on the flyleaf, but who gives a stuff what he'd written? Big, brave, fat, loser, gunning down a defenceless musician.

My dad and brother joined us, so did Sue's parents, and Julia's mother. We mumbled, murmured, shed tears in stunned disbelief, and drank tea laced with whisky. A huge hole opened in all of our lives, a hole that would never be filled.

Simon, Sue, Alan and I flew to New York for the funeral. Like most funerals, it was a lousy affair, officiated over by a Catholic priest who had never met Julia and kept waffling on about her flawed life and God's infinite forgiveness. I sighed, Sue shook her head, Barr boy scowled audibly. The Nordic nonentities who had replaced us in the band prattled on about how they'd helped Julia realise her dream and then Krauss got up to give a talk that was largely about himself. None of the original Moonbirds were asked to speak. None of Julia's strengths were mentioned. Not the fact that she was a pioneer in a male-dominated world nor that she'd pulled herself out of the deep trough of depression after the death of her father. Freddie wasn't mentioned once! None of her beliefs – not that she was anti-war, marched in the moratoriums and had a deep love for her native land. Her music was barely addressed. Her amazing life was lumped under the pathetic label of 'flawed', for Christ's sake! At least her last wish was respected – she wanted her ashes to be scattered over Tower Hill.

Three cats raced up to greet us when we stepped through the front door of Julia's apartment. Sue and I knelt down to pat them. They followed us everywhere. The next thing that struck us was that practically everything in the apartment was white: the sofas, the tables, the chairs, the beds, even Julia's piano and several guitars.

When we stood by the window in her white bedroom that looked out over Central Park, Krauss told us how Julia joyously loved to discover any hint of a change in the seasons. They had no garden to speak of, just a tiny courtyard with a fat laughing Buddha and a mini waterfall trickling over white pebbles. There was a Buddha in practically every room. Barr boy chuckled that Julia had finally become a hippy after all.

'Spiritual, Alan, spiritual,' insisted Sue, whose paintings were in every one of her friend's rooms.

Julia's lounge was dominated by Sue's paintings of the desert country of South Australia. What killed me, though, was the painting Julia had hung in the room she used to compose in, and I gave Sue a hug when she sobbed.

It was her painting of schoolchildren posing for a school photo at Portmagee Primary in the 60s. Julia and Sue knelt together on the asphalt with beaming looks on their young faces as they held up the class sign. Our original guitarist, Alex Fitzsimmons, was up the back with his tongue protruding through the gap in his front teeth. Steve stood in the second row, puffing his chest out defiantly like a pigeon. Richard was next to him, gangly and unsure of himself. Simon and I sat in the front – Moonface was radiant, I was disorientated (which is accurate, because I hated primary school). Alan Barr was up on the right-hand side with his school tie cut short by scissors. All the other kids were our childhood friends. The teacher was an old 50s rocker, a very happy Freddie, standing there proudly with his banjo.

'It's one of my oldies,' Sue smiled. 'I painted that at school while you guys were on your first tour. Julia adored it, so I gave it to her.'

We asked Krauss if we could take it back home. When he replied in the negative, we offered to buy it back, but he said, 'Zis is obviously very important history. It meant a lot to Julia so I vill keep it in the family, zen give it to the children ven zey are old enough to appreciate it.'

'Fuck it, Krauss. Your joint is full of Sue's paintings. Can't you at least spare us one?' our drummer asked.

'No, no, I must insist, because zis…'

'Yeah, yeah, get fucked,' Barr boy replied.

We didn't notice Krauss's response but we didn't care any more. We never saw the kids while we were in New York, for they were staying with family friends. Krauss didn't want them to attend Julia's funeral because he thought they were too young. In a roundabout way, I agreed with him.

Little Sue was the spitting image of Julia. When her mother's ashes were scattered from the highest tor of Tower Hill, I saw the Easter Island look of the Douglas girls in her features as the little girl sucked her fingers and cradled her furry possum hand puppet. With his red hair and blue eyes, Sean looked nothing like Krauss. When the boy stared up into the sky and smiled at two eagles circling the sun, Sue whispered that he resembled me.

For the first time since her death, I sensed Julia's spirit. She was here with her long mane of hair blowing in the wind and her brown eyes gleaming as she smiled down on us all. She'd grabbed Freddie's outstretched hand and was now calling high up in the great blue dome of the Southern Ocean sky.

Krauss told me that the breeze changed direction to brush his troubled brow when he tossed her ashes up and that he was sure her remains were born across the Pacific to America. I shrugged but gave him a sympathetic teary look.

After the ceremony, Sue, Simon and I showed the children the parts of the town that had been important to their mother. Little Sue was largely silent and clutched Krauss's hand, whereas Sean took in everything and asked a score of questions. He had his mother's enquiring mind.

All of Portmagee turned up for her wake in the Caledonian. For practically the first time in her life, Eve argued in public against Krauss that her grandchildren would be safer being raised in Australia but needless to say Krauss took the two back with him to New York. Before he flew off, he left a suitcase outside the front door of Cooinda. It was full of cassette tapes of Julia's unreleased music, some of them encrusted with blood.

29

And in the end

We got shivers up and down our spine when we heard her voice. Most of the songs were Julia singing and playing acoustic guitar by herself. Krauss had already released a posthumous album, most of it the music they'd been working on in the weeks before her death. It had his fingerprints all over it, being techno, polished and funky. It went straight to number one.

The tapes we were given were obviously older and I was all at sea on how to go about enhancing them. Did they need improving? Couldn't these hauntingly raw tapes be released just as they were? When Simon saw me agonising, he told me they needed to be polished. He proposed that we treat it as if Julia had gone on holidays and asked us to finish them off. So we pulled out our guitars, rang Steve, Mike Wotzitski and Tim Keays, packed a few bags of dope, motored up to Melbourne and began recording a new Moonbirds album. We rang Barr boy but he told us he and Helen were bonking each other silly. I kissed the bloodstained tapes; some of them were in a bad way. Julia's normally resonant voice sounded far away, but with Simon and Tim's joint knowledge, the problem was soon ironed out.

Julia wrote songs about her children, about the south-west coast and the craziness of modern existence and relationships. Curiously enough, the songs didn't mention Krauss, but talked instead of the boy from the south coast who would remain forever young. My heart was in my mouth all the time we worked on the tapes; transforming Julia's music was like conversing with a ghost. Alan's suspicions were correct: it looked as if she'd kept writing while raising Sean and Sue, but then hadn't created anything for a couple of years. Was it because she was too busy raising the kids, or that she didn't care any more? We'll probably never know.

A few biographies have appeared but they don't go into this part of her life in any great detail. I think the darling suffered another bout of depression. All the signs were there – her desire to become invisible, her inability to pursue what she truly loved. Krauss is useless, of course, and like all Stalinists he's airbrushing Julia's history. All of her solo film clips have been re-edited to give him more prominence. They're horrid now because he's figuring there in the background, sometimes in the foreground, making stupidly obscure artistic gestures. He's now claiming he was responsible for the words to some of her greatest songs.

Am I doing the same thing? When I set out to tell this story, it was with the idea that I'd romanticise the only woman that I ever loved. But Julia grabbed my hand to force me to write about the darker side of our nature, including drugs, death and depression. I wanted to write a happy tome but Julia became a part of me and demanded that I tell her story warts and all.

We simply called the last Moonbirds work *The Anthology*. It went to number one all around the world. Even though Julia was dead, there were requests that we re-form and tour but we couldn't do it, especially not for the money because it just seemed disrespectful to her spirit.

There were even strong rumours going around that we'd re-form for the Sydney Olympics. By then, Sean would be sixteen. He showed up recently in Cooinda with the schooldays painting we all loved. He reckons he pinched it without grouse Krauss's permission. Like mother, like son. God bless him!

If you come to Portmagee, have a few sherbets at the Caledonian and see a couple of chubby old bearded farts playing on the occasional Saturday. It's me and Simon. On New Year's Eve, what's left of the Moonbirds still play on the second-last float of the parade. The skinny, young, dark-haired awkward lead singer with black sunglasses is our daughter – Sue's and mine. Sue alas, is no longer with us. Those headaches she kept having were the result of a tumour that formed after she fell of the horse when she was a girl. The surgeons managed to remove it but not before it spat several other tumours throughout her body, too many and too small to be treated by chemotherapy.

Sue and I lived together in Cooinda for thirteen years and she painted right up to her death. With her gentle, inquisitive mind, her artistic nature and shared history of Julia, we understood each other totally. She was my soul sister. I couldn't have lived with anyone else. Her paintings are well known throughout Australia and are increasingly popular in London and New York.

Curiously enough, old Lloyd Rutledge's ghost vanished when she died. Like Julia, Sue had an intuitive knowledge of those who exist beside our everyday world. She now lies in the Portmagee Cemetery with the families. Barr boy is there too. He had a stroke, rumoured to be on the nest with Helen, who must be one hell of a woman!

They all look out to sea, the shore our ancestors crawled out of millions of years ago. The sea that gave us the King women and restored Julia's mind when she was on the verge of madness, the reminder that there is a life force that laps on irrespective of our petty concerns.

Simon and I still tread the sand in search of inspiration. We watch the moonbirds circle the Pacific with equinox precision and we listen to Julia's voice as she echoes the moods of the sea. If you listen quietly in the remote areas of the Western District, a spirit song will pierce your heart with the realisation that you're part of a story that began with hand paintings on a cave wall and will move on when our poor old Earth turns into a cinder.

And when the breeze brushes your wrinkled brow, perhaps it's a recently deceased loved one telling you you're not alone.